PRAISE FOR JAMES MELVILLE'S
THE DEATH CEREMONY

D0043118

Fawcett Crest Books
by James Melville:

THE CHRYSANTHEMUM CHAIN

A SORT OF SAMURAI

THE NINTH NETSUKE

DEATH OF A DAIMYO

SAYONARA, SWEET AMARYLLIS

THE DEATH CEREMONY

THE DEATH CEREMONY

James Melville

FAWCETT CREST • NEW YORK

茶道殺人事件

AUTHOR'S NOTE

There are a number of tea ceremony schools in Japan, each headed by a hereditary Grand Master. Hyogo is an actual prefecture, and its police force is based in the city of Kobe. The Japanese Ministry of Foreign Affairs maintains a liaison office in Osaka, and British diplomats and consular officers are based in Tokyo and Osaka. I should therefore like to stress that all the characters in this book are entirely fictional and bear no relation to any living person.

Prologue

THE ANGLES HAD BEEN SO PRECISELY CALCULATED THAT it was of little consequence that the actual target would be invisible. The dimensions of the room were well-known: diagrams and photographs had been published more than once. The small rectangles in the latticed wood and paper *shoji* screen formed an excellent grid for the marksman: and the laser sight on his rifle would ensure that there was no mistake.

It was now just a question of getting the timing right. There would be a tolerance of perhaps a second: plenty of time for an expert. He was filled with a fierce, holy pride at having been given this opportunity to serve, and was confident that all would go well. It seemed a lifetime since he had felt such an ecstatic clenching of the spirit, such a sense of absolute conviction as to the rightness of what he was about to do. He would not, could not miss.

It would not be long now, though in any case he experienced no impatience. He had gone beyond place and time; stepped out into a void which was a focusing of his whole being. It would be no more necessary consciously to aim

1

the rifle than it is for a Zen archer to direct his shaft. It would be as though an invisible tendril would extend from the target to the bullet, drawing it inexorably home. Failure was inconceivable.

He was unaware that he smiled.

Chapter 1

SUPERINTENDENT TETSUO OTANI LEANED FORWARD and opened his mouth to speak to his driver. He was about to say "You'd better let us out at the corner, Tomita," but stopped himself as a uniformed police inspector stepped from the side of the road into their path and saluted smartly as Tomita brought the car to a halt. Otani pressed the switch at his elbow and the window slid down.

"A Happy New Year, and welcome to Kyoto, sir. The Commander of the Prefectural Police presents his compliments, and regrets that he is unable to greet you personally. A special parking place has been reserved for your car, sir. Your driver will be directed after he has set you and your lady down."

Being in plain clothes Otani did not return the salute, but nodded instead in appreciation. "A Happy New Year to you too. You are most kind. A beautiful day. Please don't trouble too much over us. I'm sure you and your officers have many VIPs to take care of."

"A number of distinguished Japanese like yourself, sir, and two foreign ambassadors. The first tea ceremonies of

3

the new year are always big events, but we have plenty of experience of that sort of thing in Kyoto.'' The young man permitted himself a smile as he saluted again and stepped aside, and Hanae smiled back at him as their Toyota Police Special moved off and swept round the corner towards the main entrance of one of the most prestigious schools of the tea ceremony in Japan.

Hanae Otani was in the highest of spirits herself, and only wished that her husband were in a better humour. She had complimented him on his appearance before they left their house in Kobe's suburban Mount Rokko area, and indeed he looked calm and dignified in the newest and most expensive of his four dark suits, a new white shirt and the tie given to him by the Master of St Cuthbert's College, Cambridge, which he treasured above any other item in his wardrobe and wore only on very special occasions.

But then it *was* a special occasion, and they had both been taken by surprise when the invitation arrived. True, Superintendent Otani was a prominent public official in Kobe, but hardly of the status or profession which might be thought likely to gain them entrée into the most exclusive circles of Kyoto society. His late father, old Professor Otani of Osaka University, had hobnobbed with such people in his later years, after the war, and when the ostracism and worse which he had previously suffered on account of his dangerously liberal ideas had been replaced by fawning respect; but that was quite another matter.

As the great day drew near Hanae's mood of pleased anticipation had been tinged with more than a little anxiety at the prospect of spending close on two hours in the company of a number of ladies whose social and economic standing was very much more elevated than her own. Now, however, she was honest enough with herself to realise that her heavy cream silk kimono, with the discreet touches of dusty pink and gold at the sleeves and hem, was perfect for the occasion.

4

The cream and gold were festive, yet of a restrained dignity entirely seemly for a handsome matron of her age, while the pink hinted with charming subtlety at the prospect of the first plum blossom in the weeks to come. The wife of the head of the Hyogo Prefectural Police Force might not command the esteem or the bank balance of an ambassador's lady or of some of the leaders of Kyoto society, but Hanae doubted if they would be able to fault her on grounds of appearance, at least.

There were several policemen on duty outside the entrance, as well as a number of ushers or marshals in black suits with green and white armbands, all waving officiously. A glossy limousine was ahead of them, and Otani thought he recognised the slight, sprightly figure and full head of silver hair of one of Japan's leading industrialists as he stepped out and made his way through the ancient, much-photographed thatched gateway, followed at a decorous distance by his wife.

"It looks more like a funeral than a party," Otani muttered to Hanae. "All those men are just getting in the way of the police." Hanae gave him a sideways look, unsure whether he was in fact still in a tetchy mood or whether the drive to Kyoto along the Kobe–Nagoya highway had cheered him up at all. It was not that their house guest Rosie Winchmore was anything but friendly and chirpy, but there could be no doubt that she disrupted the tranquillity of the Otani household quite remarkably.

In reply to Otani's first complaints, which began when they received Rosie's letter, Hanae had teasingly pointed out that it was he who had invited her in the first place, while they were staying with their daughter Akiko and her businessman husband in London. Rosie had been their baby-sitter, a third-year student of Japanese at the School of Oriental and African Studies, and it was quite true that, flushed with the fuss that had been made of him at Cambridge and several glasses of College madeira, Otani had in a rash moment urged her to visit them in Japan.

As the day of Rosie's arrival drew near, Hanae had changed her tactics, pointing out that at least Rosie wasn't bringing her bearded bus-conductor lover with her; and that she would after all be with them for only a little over a week before going on to a short intensive course in spoken Japanese at Nanzan University in Nagoya, where she would be in the company of a group of fellow students and at a safe distance from the Otanis.

Rosie had actually arrived from Tokyo two days earlier, and Otani's nerves were already in shreds. Hanae met her at New Kobe Station, and the sight of her luggage made Hanae feel a little faint as Rosie struggled on to the platform from the sleek blue and ivory bullet-train festooned with carrier bags on the point of collapse, wearing an enormous red backpack and bearing a mysterious cardboard box from which she would not allow herself to be separated, even during the taxi ride to Rokko. The box turned out to contain a variety of health foods, mostly in unlabelled plastic bags, with which Rosie proposed to supplement those elements of the Otani diet which she expected to be able to eat.

Now she was ensconced in the little room which Akiko had occupied as a girl, and Otani was far from happy about it. Only that morning he had grumbled to Hanae about the two pairs of knickers hung to dry on the corner of the bathroom cabinet where he kept his razor and shaving cream.

The moment Otani's devoted driver Tomita stopped the car, both passenger doors at the back were wrenched open simultaneously, each by one of the marshals in question. Hanae had long since mastered the tricky art of alighting from a car in the confining folds of a kimono without revealing more than a glimpse of ankle, but it took her a little time. She was in any case sitting on the other side of

6

the car, and by the time she joined her husband, Otani was sniffing the air appreciatively as he looked at the big car now rounding the corner.

"That must be the British Ambassador arriving," he said. "Look, there's a British flag on the front. My word, a white Rolls-Royce! There aren't too many of those in Japan, I imagine." Before their visit to Britain it is most unlikely that Otani would have recognised a Union Jack; or for that matter taken the slightest interest in the sight of a Rolls-Royce, whatever its colour. Hanae was encouraged by the thought that he seemed to be cheering up.

It would have been ill-bred to stare, so Hanae urged her husband on, and they made their way along a short path of flat stones set in gravel and bordered by velvety moss to the main entrance, where they stepped out of their footwear onto the highly polished wooden step inside, and Otani was given a numbered receipt by the old attendant who stowed his shoes and Hanae's *zori* sandals in a large rack in the porch.

Then there was a brief delay while Otani knelt at the low reception desk to one side of the inner entrance, handed over their cash offering in its ceremonial envelope and wrote their names and his title in the visitors' book. It was a beautiful book, of the finest handmade paper bound in silk brocade, and Hanae watched Otani as he put on his glasses and concentrated on the task. Although far from being a scholarly man, he had a stylish way with the brush, and the results were nothing to be ashamed of.

By the time he had finished, the large foreigner who must be the British Ambassador had followed them up the freshly watered path and reached the door. He was tall, gangling and tensely awkward in his movements, giving the impression of being about to bump into something even when no obstacle presented itself, and appeared to Hanae, as she managed a discreet backward look at them, to be complaining about something to the lady who must be his wife. She was small, dark and anxious-looking, with a pinched face and a fixed, strained expression halfway between a smile and the look of one who is bravely trying not to notice an unpleasant odour. In the half-second she allowed herself, Hanae also took in the unevenness of the hem of the British lady's drab coat and the peculiar mangy strip of fur wrapped around her shoulders weighed down on one side by the unfortunate animal's head.

Then Hanae and Otani were urged through a series of low corridors towards a waiting-room where upwards of half a dozen people were already assembled. It seemed quite a crowd, but after many polite hesitations they managed to find places on the strip of felt on the *tatami* mats near a huge ceramic bowl placed in the centre of the room.

This was two-thirds full of fine ash, on top of which a few pieces of live charcoal glowed dully through their coating of powdery silver. This *hibachi* provided the only form of heating in the chilly room which obviously never saw the sun, but it was comforting and reminded Hanae of her childhood to stretch out a hand and flex her fingers over the slight but penetrating warmth coming from the charcoal. The Otanis saw nobody they knew. They had not expected to, but it was nevertheless embarrassing for them as Japanese to be in a social context with others without anybody there to introduce them during a waiting period which might easily last half an hour.

Hanae and Otani had had some slight disagreement about what was the correct time to arrive in response to an invitation which specified 1 P.M. In all day-to-day situations their obligation would have been quite clear, namely to arrive by 12.55. However, like virtually all Japanese women of her generation and social background, Hanae had as a young woman gone through a course of training in the tea ceremony. She had also taken lessons in flower arrangement, and had secured the diplomas without which her marriage prospects would have been distinctly dim. In her day the third paper qualification for finding a husband of the right type, namely a driving licence, had not yet become as important as it did in the sixties and later.

Hanae therefore knew that a period of waiting, to encourage composure of mind and spirit, was regarded as an essential component of a formal tea ceremony, and that the higher the rank of the person performing it, the longer the wait tended to be. If Sen-no-Rikyu, the sixteenth-century founder of the institutionalised "way of tea", could keep the dictator of Japan waiting and make him humble himself by creeping through an entrance made deliberately low and difficult to negotiate, his twentieth-century successors as masters of the various schools derived from Rikyu's teaching were justified in applying the same principles.

Honoured and surprised as they had both been to receive an invitation in the name of the Iemoto, the head of the house or Grand Master himself, and more than willing to drive forty miles in each direction on a Sunday to be present, Hanae for her part was dubious about the philosophy of waiting, or hanging about, as she put it more bluntly to her husband. She had suggested that to arrive at about twenty past one would be perfectly satisfactory, being quite convinced that the actual ceremony was most unlikely to begin before one forty-five or even two o'clock.

Otani did not agree, and they had arrived on the stroke of one. Now, kneeling quietly by Hanae's side, he leant across to her under the pretence of shifting his position slightly and murmured that he was sure they had done the right thing, for had not the British Ambassador who must surely be the guest of honour arrived hard on their heels?

The arrival at their house of Rosie Winchmore in response to his ill-considered invitation had muted Otani's recent anglophile mood considerably, but the sight of the white Rolls-Royce with the gaudy little flag fluttering from its standard had brought on a momentary surge of sentiment, and he tried to make allowances for the ambassador

9

and his lady who now entered the room, he in full spate of voluble but quaintly accented Japanese, she meek and silent in his turbulent wake.

"Thank you. Ah! This way, is it? Come along, Thelma, oh, splendid, there's Takayama-san!" He had spotted the industrialist, sitting complacently cross-legged by the hibachi. "Happy New Year, Takayama-san!" the ambassador boomed, his glasses flashing keenly round the room as he searched for other acquaintances. "You've met my wife, of course. And there's your good lady. Happy New Year to you, madam," he added to Hanae, who happened to be nearest to the famous tycoon on his other side. Hanae made a small gesture of disclaimer as the true Mrs Takayama bowed low and murmured a stream of courteous greetings.

Only slightly abashed, the ambassador glared briefly at Otani as though the mistake had been his fault, and began talking again. "A thousand pardons. Rather dark in here, isn't it? Hurtling is my name. British Ambassador. Look, Takayama-san, I suppose this isn't the time or place, but we ought to have a word about the Merseyside project. It's really high time your people came to a decision, and you know as well as I do that the union problem isn't anything like as bad as the Press here has been implying." More people in the room than he might have supposed understood as he switched briefly to English. "Thelma, remind me to do a lunch for some newspaper presidents in Tokyo again, though I must say I might just as well talk to a brick wall."

He bumbled through the room as he talked, and although in stockinged feet like everyone else, managed to tread on Otani's ankle as he passed. Takayama had not yet said a word, but there was a slight twist at one corner of his thin, sardonic mouth, and one eyebrow was raised perceptibly higher than the other as he contrived to find space for the big Englishman and his crushed-looking wife. The other Japanese guests had been listening to the ambassador's

10

monologue with open curiosity, none more intrigued than Otani. There was no doubt that the man could speak Japanese, nor that it was the Japanese of an educated person; but the blurting, machine-gun style of delivery and apparent obliviousness to the reactions of those around him struck Otani as being not so much alien as almost unbelievable.

It soon became disappointingly clear that Takayama, a past master of the art of neutralising hostile television interviewers, was not to be drawn on the subject of his company's much-publicised delay in deciding whether or not to invest tens of millions of pounds in a new factory in Britain. When the ambassador at last fell briefly silent, the industrialist greeted him in the conventional way, then firmly enquired after the health of Mrs Margaret Thatcher and of the member of her government who had recently visited Japan in yet another attempt to lean on him and his senior colleagues.

Otani caught Hanae's eye and she raised a hand quickly to conceal her smile. The ambassador was generating such a hubbub that she could safely have whispered a comment to her husband, but at that moment a new disturbance was caused by the arrival of yet more guests in the now quite crowded room. These were no less a personage than the Governor of Kyoto Prefecture and his wife, closely followed by a resplendent black couple in colourful robes who beamed fatly round at the assembled company with such refulgent goodwill that even the most inhibited of the Japanese guests responded with shy smiles.

With the best will in the world, no room could possibly be found for them all to sit, but relief was at hand. Just as the other guests began to half-scramble up in deference to the Governor and his lady, a senior usher appeared at the door and with the most profuse apologies indicated that they should all now proceed to the tea ceremony room.

Like the Governor's wife, Hanae patted her hair-do and adjusted her *obi* sash for reassurance and then demurely

11

followed her husband along more corridors open to one side to give fleeting views of meticulously groomed inner gardens. It was quite a relief to be on the move again and away from the immediate proximity of the explosive voice of the British Ambassador, but she found herself wondering how on earth getting on for twenty people could possibly be fitted into a classic tea ceremony room with a floor space of four and a half tatami mats each roughly two square yards in extent.

The room to which the guests were led was, however, not of this type, being altogether larger and loftier, at least twenty mats in size and much more like those found in Japanese restaurants of the most exclusive and expensive kind. It was a room of great beauty and Hanae realised at once that nothing but the finest traditional materials had been used in its construction. The woodwork was of *hinoki*, glowing like honey and subtly setting off the rich golden sheen of the tatami mats edged with plain black cloth. In the *tokonoma* alcove the only decoration was an ancient scroll mounted on silk.

At first it seemed dark in the room, but the eye soon became adjusted to the subdued light filtering through the translucent paper of the shoji screens, and it was possible to see a wisp of steam emerging from the lid of the cauldron in the square *kotatsu* pit not far from the tokonoma, in front of the sliding *fusuma* doors through which the Grand Master would presumably make his appearance.

Before that, however, came what an uninformed observer would have taken to be a highly unseemly disturbance, as the guests struggled with every appearance of sincerity to yield precedence to each other. Otani and Hanae took no part in the mêlée, since Otani marched decisively to a point near the back wall not too far from the door and therefore well down the pecking order, and made himself comfortable on one of the flat *zabuton* cushions already in place. Hanae sank gratefully down on his left, and watched with interest the tussle going on near the to-konoma. It was obvious to her that the Governor must sooner or later take the place of honour immediately in front of it, but he was urgently pressing the industrialist Takayama to do so. Takayama for his part was modestly declining the honour, while managing to draw attention to the presence of the British Ambassador, who looked to Hanae as though he quite expected to take precedence, even though he was protesting loudly that it would be entirely inappropriate for him to do so.

All the other guests gradually sorted themselves out, in-cluding the dusky personages whom, Hanae agreed in an undertone with Otani, must be the other ambassador and his wife. It seemed for a while as though the argument among the three most distinguished guests would go on indefinitely, but all at once the Governor smiled winningly, made a graceful gesture of defeat, and plonked himself down in the place of honour. His wife, who Hanae thought had been looking rather tense and unhappy, at once took her place at his side. Takayama moved almost as fast, tak-ing the next cushion in order of precedence and leaving the ambassador like a beached whale in the middle of the room with his wife smiling round rather wildly. The only places now left unoccupied were to the left of Hanae. Although some of the other higher-ranking guests made preliminary movements suggestive of yielding their places, they were perfunctory in the extreme, and eventually the ambassador, still talking to nobody in particular, made his way across the room and sank creakingly first to his knees and then into a cross-legged position. Hanae was profoundly grate-ful for the fact that his much smaller and less obtrusive wife took the place next to her.

A hushed atmosphere now fell upon the gathering, rather as though all present were waiting for a church service to begin, and male attendants in formal Japanese dress glided in through the fusuma doors carrying lacquer trays of glu-

13

tinous bean-jelly cakes. The Japanese guests produced wads of folded thick white paper and placed one sheet in front of them on the tatami to serve as a plate. In most cases the wife had the paper tucked into the kimono folds at her breast, and passed a sheet to her husband as well, but some of the men had a personal supply in an inner pocket.

Noticing a Japanese lady on the other side of the room courteously offering paper to the black couple in the tribal robes, Hanae realised that the British pair were similarly unprovided and hastily passed two sheets to them with a nod and a smile. The ambassador thanked her noisily, drawing attention to the silence of everyone else in the room, then at last fell silent himself and followed the example of the others by attacking his bean-jelly cake with the sliver of bamboo provided and transferring lumps of it to his mouth. The attendants withdrew, closing the sliding screen door behind them. Almost at once it opened again and a distinguished figure entered the room, a single attendant close behind.

The Seventeenth Hereditary Grand Master of the Southern School of the tea ceremony proceeded gravely to his place beside the cauldron, placed the implements of bamboo and lacquer which he would employ carefully on the tatami, knelt and bowed low to his guests.

Chapter 2

HANAE KNEW THAT THE GRAND MASTER WAS AN EL-derly man; something over sixty, certainly. Yet, as he raised himself from the profound bow and his eyes flickered round the room and held hers for a fraction of a second, she was aware of an animal power in him of a distinctly sexual nature which momentarily disturbed her breathing. Hanae soon enough pulled herself together, reflecting a little ruefully that probably every other woman in the room had reacted in the same way as herself.

She always liked to see men in traditional Japanese dress anyway, and would have been happy indeed if Otani had consented to put on his own dark-blue kimono, the short outer jacket held together at the front by its splendid woven silk tasselled cord. The Grand Master's garments were of stiff silk and fell around his unexpectedly burly frame magnificently. The touch of pure white at his neck seemed to emphasise his fleshy lips, fine profile and thick grey hair.

Not a word was spoken at this stage, and the Grand Master began at once to perform the tea ceremony he must have conducted tens of thousands of times since childhood,

15

trained as he had been from infancy to inherit the headship of his family and with it responsibility for the school and its network of hundreds of licensed teachers throughout Japan.

Hanae, although herself less than reverent about the ceremony, had to admit that the Iemoto performed it with wondrously fluid dexterity: the grace with which he handled the long bamboo ladle, warming the bowl he had brought with him with water from the cauldron simmering over the charcoal, the seemingly casual way he folded and re-folded the silk square with which he ceremoniously wiped the slender bamboo spoon before scooping out the requisite quantity of powdered tea from its lacquer container, and perhaps above all the muscular authority of his handling of the whisk. All his movements took Hanae's breath away again as she remembered the trembling of her own hand and the generally gauche incompetence of her efforts when in the presence of her own teacher in Tokyo thirty-five years earlier. That teacher, too, had been a disciple of the Southern School, and Hanae remembered the prescribed movements well enough although she had not performed, or indeed even attended, a tea ceremony for years.

She found herself wondering what might be passing through the mind of the alarmingly attractive Grand Master as he performed the ritual so familiar to him, and through the minds of the other guests watching him so intently. Even the British Ambassador was still, his big ungainly shape towering a head higher than anyone else in the room; while his black counterpart gazed in fascination, his chubby face glistening.

The tea was made at last, and with a distant smile the Grand Master passed the bowl to his assistant who placed it before the guest of honour. The Governor bowed low, his hands on the tatami mat before him and his forehead almost touching them, and the Grand Master bowed in response. Then all the other guests bowed.

Afterwards Hanae swore she heard nothing apart from a rustling of clothing; not even the cracking of a knee joint which would not have been unexpected in a company of whom the youngest was well into middle age. Otani thought he did hear something, but could not be sure.

What he and all the other guests did see as they resumed an upright position, however, was the Grand Master slumped in a heap, his attendant bending over him incredulously. Otani flung himself across the room without rising properly from his knees, and was looking down at the fallen man almost before anyone else in the room fully realised that anything was amiss.

The Grand Master had toppled to one side, and without touching him, Otani came to the conclusion that he was almost certainly dead, even though little blood had emerged from the ugly wound in his forehead. Nevertheless, as he reached for the limp wrist of the uppermost arm and failed to find a pulse, he ordered the attendant to phone for an ambulance at once, and to summon the nearest uniformed policeman from outside the buildings immediately.

He tried a moment longer, but there was no response to his probing fingers. Then Otani stood and surveyed his fellow guests, some of whom were beginning to scramble to their feet. "Ladies and gentlemen. Please keep your seats for a moment. I am a police officer. The Iemoto has been injured. Medical help will arrive very soon." Then he turned to the Governor of Kyoto Prefecture, dropped to his knees in front of him and spoke in an urgent undertone, but with no real attempt at confidentiality. "Governor. Forgive me for taking action. I am Otani, commander of the Hyogo Prefectural Police. With your permission I will liaise with officers of the Kyoto force for the moment. I should be obliged if you could ensure that the ambassadors at least do not leave the premises for the time being." The Governor nodded, a look of stupefaction still on his face and Otani made without more ado for the door and into the corridor.

There was no time to retrieve his shoes from the custodian at the main entrance, so he fumbled briefly with the screw-lock of the glazed sliding wall which gave on to the side garden, wrenched it open and jumped down on to the gravel, wincing on impact. The moss was kinder to his feet, but he was soon heedless of discomfort as he rounded the side of the building in which the tea ceremony room was located and made a quick inspection of the outside of the shoji screen which had been behind him and Hanae.

The small hole he had spotted in the paper from inside was not difficult to find, and from his recollection of the layout of the room and the position of the Grand Master, Otani made a crude estimate of the probable trajectory of the bullet. Then he plunged into the dense stand of bamboo, made for the boundary wall and managed to haul himself up to its tiled top by half-climbing one of the more sturdy plants which nevertheless swayed dangerously under his weight. As he did so he heard the wailing of an ambulance approaching.

On the other side of the wall was an alley: too narrow for a vehicle larger than a motor-bike, but offering easy access to a proper road no more than fifty metres away. There was a similar wall on the other side of the alley, marking the boundary of a substantial property of an old-fashioned kind. As is usually the case in Kyoto, the house itself was practically invisible save for its roof, but the white wall of a separate fireproof storehouse with its tiny ventilation window abutted on to the wall.

The alley was deserted, and there was obviously nothing Otani could do there. He therefore climbed down from his perch and after looking carefully around and sniffing the air, made his way back through the garden, sitting on the edge of the corridor to brush the gravel and dirt from his

18

socks as best he could before going back to the tea cere-mony room, expecting to be greeted by a scene of chaos.

He had been gone less than fifteen minutes, but the room proved to be almost empty, except for the Governor, the two ambassadors, the police inspector who had greeted the Otanis on their approach to the school, and a middle-aged man in a black suit and silver tie. The inspector saluted, his face solemn. "Mihara, sir. I regret to inform you that the Iemoto was already dead when the ambulance arrived."

Otani knew he was on delicate ground. He had received the Governor's bemused consent to liaise with the Kyoto police in the emergency, but had already exceeded his brief by chasing off in a vain attempt to find some trace of the gunman. "I am distressed to hear it," he replied briefly. "Needless to say, Inspector Mihara, if I can be of any service to you . . . ah, may I ask where the other guests are?"

"In another room, sir. There was to be another tea cer-emony at three o'clock, and some of those guests were already beginning to arrive." He turned to the man in the black suit. "Mr Terada here is the Chief of the General Affairs Section of the School, and responsible for the administration of today's ceremonies. After consultation with him I have arranged for arriving guests to be informed that the later ceremony is cancelled." The man Terada nodded his assent. His face was a sickly grey colour.

The British Ambassador looked almost as ill, and the shock had left him chastened. He was standing in a corner conversing quite quietly with his black colleague and the Governor, and Otani seized the opportunity to draw the inspector to the other side of the room. "Inspector. I must apologise for having left the room before you arrived. The fact is, I think there may be more than a possibility that the Iemoto was killed by a shot intended for the British Ambassador over there. You will see a small hole in the shoji of the back wall. It is precisely at the level the ambassador's head would have been had he not been bowing at the moment when the shot was fired. I made a rough guess as to where it might have come from and hurried to see if I could find any trace of the gunman.''

"I'm very grateful to you, sir. And did you?''

"No, but of course my inspection was hasty and very superficial. The important thing is, if I may say so, to provide special protection for both ambassadors, though I doubt if there need be any concern for—who is the other one?''

"He's the Ambassador of Ghana.''

"I see. At all events, if there's anything in my idea, the assassin will soon learn that he killed the wrong man and may remain in the vicinity to make another attempt.''

Otani looked hard at the younger man, then turned aside to let him think about what he said. Mihara needed only a few seconds to digest the information Otani had provided, before turning to the administrator Terada and asking him to provide a list of the names of all the guests at the ceremony and sending him out of the room. Otani guessed that this was simply a way of getting rid of him, and was not surprised when the inspector moved quickly across to the Governor and the two ambassadors and interrupted their conversation which appeared to be in English. After listening briefly to Inspector Mihara, the Governor looked over to Otani and gestured to him to join them.

Otani went over, and took his first proper look at the Governor, who was short and portly like many another prominent politician, his enamelled badge of office gleaming in his lapel. At close quarters he seemed less impressive than his deft handling of the precedence fuss at the beginning of the ceremony had led Otani to think him, and the sweat on his forehead was very noticeable.

"I am very grateful to you for your prompt actions, Superintendent,'' he said as though very far from meaning it. "This is a shocking business. The tragic death of the Grand

Master is a terrible thing, and now the Inspector here tells me that you consider that the shot may have been aimed in fact at the British Ambassador. Sir Rodney Hurtling had just been hazarding the same suggestion." Otani puzzled over the sounds *Saa Rodoni Haatoringu* and then concluded that they must represent the ambassador's full name. *Haatoringu* bore some slight resemblance to the word the ambassador had uttered while peremptorily introducing himself to Hanae, and thanks to his trip to England Otani had at last learned the significance of the title "Sir".

As he bowed his head in acknowledgement of the Governor's words, Otani thought that he looked completely out of his depth in an emergency situation, without advisers to guide him and menials to do his bidding. "It is, of course, purely by chance that I happen to be here today, Governor. I did however venture to suggest to Inspector Mihara that it would be prudent to arrange special protection for both their Excellencies when they leave these premises. The assailant may still be in the vicinity."

At this the British Ambassador looked round in some nervousness, and moved round so that his colourfully robed African colleague was between him and the shoji screens. "I don't know about you, Edwin," he then said to the other envoy, "but I feel I ought to return immediately to Tokyo." Then he made an impatient gesture, and turned to the Governor, changing to Japanese. "However, I can't. Perhaps Osaka would be better. I can't let my European colleagues down . . . wait a minute while I think. Of course the Rolls is safe enough. The trouble is, Governor, I have an important exhibition to open—well, jointly open, perhaps I should say—on Wednesday in Kobe, and my wife and I had planned to stay here in Kyoto tonight and tomorrow. It's all rather difficult."

His words were quite comprehensible to Otani, but the ambassador's thought processes were beginning to make his head spin slightly. He therefore gently intervened.

"May I suggest, Governor—subject of course to Inspector Mihara's advice—that His Excellency might proceed by car to his hotel under escort? I gather from the ambassador's remarks that the vehicle is bullet-proof . . ."

"Who told you that?" Sir Rodney Hurtling's eyes flashed at Otani, dark suspicion in his manner.

"Why, you did, Ambassador. At least you implied as much." Otani's adrenalin levels were still high, and he had no intention of allowing this boorish man to browbeat him.

"Did I? Oh. Anyway, you're a senior police officer, I'm told. Still, the information isn't for general consumption, you know. You advise that, do you?"

The man was obviously still dithering, and Otani decided to be charitable. "You've had a serious shock, Ambassador," he suggested kindly. "You will no doubt need to confer by telephone with your staff at the Embassy . . ."

"You're right, you know. He's right, Governor. Thelma—that's Lady Hurtling, of course—Thelma's in something of a state. It's a good thing we're staying at the Miyako, they have a proper drill for VIP protection. You'll remember, Governor, the Prince of Wales stayed there, in sixty-eight I think it was, before your time, of course. We generally go to one of the inns at Nanzenji when we come to Kyoto, they've known me for years at the Kikusui, but this time it's quite true, as the Superintendent here points out, we're at the Miyako."

Otani looked at Inspector Mihara, who nodded in response and moved forward to address the two ambassadors. "If you will come this way, Your Excellencies, we will arrange for your cars to be called at once. I can detach men on motorcycles to escort you to your hotels." Otani could not understand his English but it sounded stilted, not like that of his own trusted assistant Kimura.

The black man beamed. "Don't worry about me, Inspector," he rumbled. "Nobody after me. Not in Japan, anyway. Just at home." He chuckled fruitily and slapped
22

Sir Rodney on the back. "You just take care of Sir Rodney here."

"As you wish, Your Excellency." Mihara turned to the Governor and reverted with evident relief to Japanese. "Governor, may I have your authority to arrange for plainclothes officers to provide a security watch at the hotel?"

"Yes, yes. Do that." The Governor seemed to fear, probably rightly, that he was being taken for granted and now began to take ostentatious command, urging Hurtling and the Ghanaian forward towards the door.

Otani was the last to leave the room, and, as he did so, held back to take a last look round. Swiftly crossing to the spot where the Grand Master had been kneeling when shot, he glanced down at the tatami. The blood had soaked through the woven grass surface of the tatami leaving little trace behind, but the sight of the lacquer tea container on its side, its lid having rolled free and a small quantity of powdered tea having spilled, was somehow even more shockingly disturbing, as was the disorder of the cushions discarded by the guests as they had hurriedly left or been shepherded from the room. Otani had not been told what they had done with the body, and had little curiosity about it. There would of course be an autopsy, and the bullet would no doubt be recovered from the victim's skull. It might prove to be of some value in the investigation, but then again it might not.

He looked round the room again. Something was troubling him, but he could not put a finger on it, and after musing without effect for a while he made his way back to the waiting-room in search of Hanae.

At the sight of her husband she rose eagerly from her kneeling position beside the massive bowl of the hibachi with a smile. Then her eyes widened as she looked him up and down and the words came out in a suppressed wail.

23

"Darling . . . that was your *best suit*!" Otani's mouth twitched as he looked at her. He had noted her use of the past tense.

Chapter 3

"**S**O I THOUGHT I OUGHT TO LET YOU KNOW, EVEN though it won't be a matter for us, of course. I was not unimpressed by the senior Kyoto man on the spot. Mihara his name was." Otani leant back comfortably in his chair and surveyed his two colleagues. The winter sun sent a shaft of brilliance across one corner of the big, shabby old office and showed up the frayed areas here and there on the venerable brown linoleum which Kimura regularly urged him to have replaced with the smart new-style carpet tiles he had specified for his own cubby-hole of an office on the ground floor.

Although it was already the eighth of January, this was their first extended meeting since the New Year holidays which legally consist of New Year's Day only, but which, in strict practice, extend over at least the next two days while all banks and commercial offices are closed, and by immemorial custom for most people peter out only around the fifth or sixth of the month with the round of New Year parties and inspiring speeches by company presidents and lesser bosses to their staff. Otani had indeed himself only

25

recently addressed a gathering of his headquarters officers: he had not much enjoyed it and was glad that he could now revert to his normal unobtrusive routine, seeing only a handful of his senior colleagues at all frequently. Of those, Kimura had a significant part of his confidence, while Noguchi had virtually all of it.

Inspector Jiro Kimura, chief of the External Affairs Section, was conventionally tailored that day, in a dark-blue pinstripe suit, pale-blue shirt and knitted blue tie. His fingers were laced delicately round one knee, and the gleaming polish of the shoe poised in mid-air reflected the sunlight. "I've heard of Mihara," he now conceded judiciously. "As a matter of fact, he's my opposite number there. Needless to say, he has only a handful of foreign residents to worry about compared with my people in the Kobe area."

Otani smiled briefly. "I may say that he looked very smart, Kimura-kun. In uniform." Otani looked up at the ceiling as he continued. "Whatever became of the uniform I'm told you wore while I was away in England?"

There was a snort from the third man in the room and Otani transferred his gaze to him blandly. "Come, come, Ninja," he chided him. "The last—and come to think of it the *only* time I ever saw you in uniform was in 1964 when you were Divisional Inspector for the harbour police and you took the Mayor on an inspection tour. Nearly drowned him, too, didn't you?"

"Wish I had. What put it into your head to go to Kyoto anyway?"

"Ninja" Noguchi had known Otani too long to rise to his occasional teasing in the way that the much younger Kimura invariably did, and as Otani's senior in age by several years had the privilege of saying whatever he liked to him. Although not very tall, he looked like a cross between a retired *sumo* wrestler and a day labourer. Inspector Hachiro Noguchi, chief of the Drugs Section, was already over retirement age, and Otani was waging a so far successful battle to keep him in harness. His latest communication to the Personnel Division of the National Police Agency, who wanted to send a man in his late forties from Nagasaki, had countered their offer with a proposal to retire Noguchi formally but give him the status of full-time "consultant", and Otani reflected with satisfaction that it would take them at least six months even to think about that one, much less say yea or nay to it.

That day, Noguchi was wearing his usual grimy and capacious trousers, once the lower half of a suit, secured to his bulging belly by a vast leather belt which looked as though it had once formed part of the harness of a carthorse. Over a faded blue shirt minus a collar, he wore a tattered cardigan in a startling design of multi-coloured diamonds.

"I told you. We were invited. It's quite an honour, you know, Ninja. I must admit that I probably wouldn't have bothered on my own account, but I didn't want to disappoint my wife . . ." This was an outrageous misrepresentation of the true state of affairs, since Otani had been only too glad to have a cast-iron excuse to escape from the house at Rokko for the best part of a day during Rosie Winchmore's stay, while Hanae for her part had been initially quite cool about the prospect. Moreover, she had pointed out that they would have to take a monetary gift with them and that this could not decently be less than ten thousand yen, representing housekeeping money for at least two days, possibly three with luck. They had in the end presented fifteen thousand, since the Grand Master himself was to officiate.

"Bit of excitement for you, anyway, guy getting killed like that." Noguchi raised a massive hand to refuse a refill of his cup of green tea as Otani replenished his own from the old tin kettle on the battered tray and pointed it enquiringly at his two lieutenants. Noguchi had barely touched his first cup, but then he hardly ever did. Kimura's watch suddenly emitted a series of bleeps, and he hastily fumbled at it, trying several of the numerous buttons before managing to silence it.

Otani raised an eyebrow quizzically, but made no comment. "It was certainly unexpected," he said to Noguchi. "And an extraordinary way to plan an assassination. What still bothers me is how it was conceived. How the fellow aimed, I mean. There was no source of light within the room to produce shadows against the shoji paper, and certainly no video camera anywhere that I could see . . . in any case, it's inconceivable that anyone could have rigged one there without the staff of the place knowing. Then again, how could he know where the ambassador would be sitting? It was in doubt right to the last minute." Otani sighed rather disconsolately. "Anyway, it's obviously a matter for the Kyoto force. I suppose I might have to submit a statement, but that's all. Now, gentlemen, we must think about our work. We have a full meeting of all section chiefs this afternoon, and I just want your views on one or two of the matters likely to come up, so that I'll have a good idea of the consensus I ought to steer people to . . ."

The next hour passed satisfactorily enough, and it was noon and time to think about lunch almost before Otani realised it. At the end of their conference he asked Kimura and Noguchi if either of them had brought a boxed lunch they might wish to fetch to join him for his own midday meal, but neither had. No interest was ever expressed by anyone in headquarters about Noguchi's private plans, and he melted away in his customary disconcerting style. The minor mystery of Kimura's unusually sober rig was cleared up when he volunteered that he had a lunch appointment with one of the staff of the American Consulate-General, adding hastily that it was strictly business, and promising without fail to be back in time for the staff meeting at three.

Left to himself, Otani went over to his desk and retrieved his own lunch-box from the top of the small filing cabinet to one side, where he had placed it under that morning's edition of the *Kobe Shimbun* to protect it from the sun. It was a simple affair of black lacquer, which had once belonged to his father, the stiff-necked old scientist who had so deplored his only son's failure to follow in his academic footsteps. The original quality of the lacquer had been so good, and it had been so lovingly cared for, that it still looked beautiful, and Otani always took it into his hands with satisfaction mingled with a touch of curiosity over what Hanae would have put in it for him that day.

''Something from the mountains and something from the sea'' had become their catch-phrase at home since reading the run-away best-seller about Totto-chan, the little girl at the window whose early education at a uniquely liberal experimental school near Tokyo before and during the Second World War had so caught the imagination of the Japanese public. The enlightened headmaster's insistence that the lunch-boxes of his charges should contain these essential elements summed up Hanae's instinctive thinking anyway, she was pleased to realise.

Quite often the snowy bed of cooked rice which usually occupied one-third of the space inside had a pickled plum in the centre, making a symbolic *hinomaru* rising sun, like the Japanese flag. Then in addition there was generally a morsel of grilled fish or perhaps a shrimp, as well as burdock, some *tofu* and inevitably pickles. Otani always looked forward to lunch-box days.

He took a pair of throwaway chopsticks in their paper wrapper from the packet he now kept in one of his desk drawers, having decided quite arbitrarily one day that the washable lacquer kind he had always previously used were unhygienic, even though he still ate with them quite happily at home. Then he bore box and chopsticks over to the low coffee-table and resumed the seat he had occupied earlier while talking to Kimura and Noguchi.

He removed the lid and stopped short, frozen in the act of laying it down beside the box, and stared aghast at his lunch. The tofu was there. There was also a piece of pumpkin, and three neat cylinders of cooked spinach next to some perfectly ordinary marinaded squid. It was the rice that filled Otani with horror. It was *brown*.

Chapter 4

"**I** DON'T CARE *WHAT* SHE THINKS," OTANI SAID HOTLY, "I want proper rice from now on. *White* rice." He was speaking in a passionate undertone to Hanae as she prepared their evening meal in the kitchen to the accompaniment of sploshing sounds and tuneless singing from the bathroom where, Otani had said to Hanae, it sounded as though Rosie Winchmore was not so much taking a bath as doing somersaults in it. Hanae tried to calm him down.

"She means well, darling. I've tried to explain to her, and I think she understands now that she shouldn't have thrown the cooked rice in the refrigerator away. But by the time I had to get your lunch ready there was only the unpolished rice she'd brought in the house. I was hoping you might not notice . . ."

"Not *notice*? Why, it was inedible—" Otani broke off as the bathroom door was flung open and Rosie emerged, stark naked except for the small towel which is normally all that is to be found in Japanese bathrooms and which she was holding before her in a sketchy and unsuccessful attempt at modesty.

31

The vision lasted no more than half a second as she caught sight of Otani and hastily scuttled back in with a stifled scream, and Hanae, whose back had been turned, remained in ignorance of what had caused the disturbance. Otani coughed and withdrew from the kitchen. From the safe distance of the living room, he raised his voice so that Hanae could still hear him. "I think Rosie-san needs a *yukata.*" Then he sank down limply on to a cushion and closed his eyes for a moment. It was all too much. He supposed that his subordinate Kimura had naked young women all over his *manshon* flat as a regular thing, but would gladly have forgone the luxury himself. He sighed and picked up the remote-control switch of the television. It was nearly six-thirty, and he might as well look at the news, put out as he was by having been prevented by Rosie from having his own bath immediately on returning home, as was his usual custom.

It would have been out of the question to try to hush up the death of so eminent a public figure as the hereditary head of the Southern School of the tea ceremony, one of the unquestioned leaders of Kyoto society and a prominent figure in any public debate on national cultural policy. Nevertheless, the family seemed to have persuaded the Kyoto police to delay releasing the news to the media for some twenty-four hours. Otani was quite surprised at the amount of attention now given to the matter in the national network news. Although slightly more careful than the newspapers, which habitually indulged in speculation as though the concept of libel was unknown to Japanese law, the commercial TV networks were fairly nonchalant as a rule. Otani noted with interest that there was not even the most oblique reference to the theory he had himself advanced: that the British Ambassador had been the actual target. Indeed, although the presence of "distinguished Japanese and foreign guests" at the fatal tea ceremony was freely referred to, the newsreader did not name any of them.

Instead several minutes were given up to the showing of film clips of notable events in the dead man's tenure of office as Iemoto following the death of his father nearly forty years earlier. Otani watched, fascinated, as the late teacher was shown welcoming various foreign dignitaries at the entrance through which he and Hanae had passed only the previous day, and ushering them towards the group of venerable thatched buildings which were his official residence as well as the headquarters of a nation-wide organisation with international affiliates, part cult, part educational institution and part business.

There were also clips of the slain Grand Master in conference with the Prime Minister of Japan, lecturing on the aesthetics of the tea ceremony in Paris, and being awarded the key to the City of Honolulu by the Mayor, himself of Japanese ancestry. There was no doubt in Otani's mind that had it not been for his untimely death the Grand Master would, having comfortably passed the minimum qualifying age of sixty, before long have been the recipient of formal honours from the Japanese authorities; a Culture Prize at least or possibly the Order of the Chrysanthemum.

Before the announcer turned to the next subject one last picture came on to the screen. It was a still photograph of the new Iemoto, eldest son of the dead man and now eighteenth hereditary head of the Southern School. At thirty-two, it seemed he had for many years served as his father's principal lieutenant with responsibility for the school's finances and administration. Depicted dressed in a Western-style business suit, he looked the rising young executive he was; earnest, bespectacled and conventional. Otani retained only the most fleeting image of the young man as the picture changed to a gory close-up of the latest motorway crash with the camera dwelling lovingly on the blood-stained tarmac and Rosie entered the room, now decently covered in a blue and white cotton yukata, which Otani recognised as being one of Hanae's.

33

She showed no sign of lingering embarrassment as she sank down on to a cushion near Otani and he resignedly switched off the TV. "I hope you enjoyed your lunch today," she said in her halting Japanese. "I found that you can buy unpolished rice in the ordinary shop! White rice is poison, you know." She suppressed a laugh with an inelegant snort as Otani gaped at her disbelievingly. "I had a funny conversation with the old woman who served me. I asked her if she sold *gemmai* and she looked very suspicious. Then she nodded and weighed me out one kilo. Then she said, 'What are you going to do with it?' So of course I said I was going to eat it. 'Are you going to cook it first?' she asked me. Honestly!"

This time Rosie chuckled merrily as Otani sat with a perfectly straight face, quite failing to see anything to laugh at. He entirely understood and sympathised with the old lady's bewilderment that any normal person should wish to buy rice in its original state. "We don't eat rice like that," he said at length. "We don't like it." Rosie seemed in no way cast down, and Otani felt obliged to try a little harder to be sociable, but as he opened his mouth to speak Rosie forestalled him.

"Mrs Otani was upset with me for throwing away the rice in the refrigerator. Sorry. But now you've actually tried brown rice you won't want to change back, will you? It's good for the body."

The transparent sincerity and missionary zeal of the girl affected Otani in spite of himself, and he shook his head gently with a small smile. "Everyone over forty in Japan *has* tried it, Rosie-san. We ate it like that during the war, but that doesn't mean we liked it. It's impolite, I know, but I'm afraid my wife and I are too old to change our ways now . . . tell me, what have you done today?"

"Oh, I had an interesting time. I went into Kobe and took the special train to Port Island to have a look round. Then I walked around and looked at the shops and found the place where the old houses the foreigners used to live in have been restored . . .''

Otani nodded benignly enough, understanding part at least of what she was saying, but by no means everything. At least Rosie had plenty to say for herself, and the odd pronunciation and ungrammatical constructions tumbled about his ears as she rambled on happily and he reflected how different his own daughter Akiko had been at her age. The only times Akiko, as a militant Marxist student at Kobe University in the sixties, had broken her long, sullen periods of silence had been when she harangued Otani on the subject of his profession, his antediluvian attitudes to women and his criminal responsibility for propping up a rotten and corrupt social order. Otani found it odd to think that Akiko was now the occasional employer of the tousle-haired English girl sitting there in Akiko's old place in the living-room at Rokko.

"Ojama shimasu!" It was Hanae, apologetically interrupting Rosie's monologue. ''We can eat any time you like. Would you like to have your bath now?''

Otani blinked as he dragged himself back out of his reverie. ''What? Oh. No. Thank you. Let's eat by all means. I'll have my bath later.'' He had already noted with satisfaction that Rosie was reasonably helpful about the house, and she now scrambled up and helped Hanae to set the table over the kotatsu pit in the middle of the room with its low-powered electric heater in the bottom. The padded cover was already in position and it was a simple matter to place the flat square of simulated lacquer on top and set out chopsticks on their stands and the condiments; the small bottle of soy sauce and hot red *togarashi* pepper and the milder green mixed powdered *sansho* herbs in their bamboo shakers.

Hanae had cooked a delicious pork and vegetable *itame*, the ingredients half-fried, half-steamed in their own moisture in her big round Chinese-style pan, and a separate

35

vegetarian version for Rosie, with a fragrant clear soup with bamboo shoots and seaweed. Otani perked up considerably as he attacked his supper with relish, defiantly passing his bowl twice to Hanae for additional helpings of white rice as Rosie shook her head sadly over their backsliding.

Hanae was wearing a blue Western-style matching blouse and skirt while Otani was in his shirt-sleeves, so Rosie the foreigner was in fact the only one round the table in Japanese clothing. Otani was relieved to notice as Hanae asked endless questions about London, the Shimizu household and their four-year-old grandson Kazuo in particular that, notwithstanding her dietary theories, Rosie was not an abstainer from alcohol. The spare flask of *sake* kept warming in the pot of hot water at Hanae's side had to be replenished several times during the hour they sat there, and Rosie certainly consumed her fair share.

Indeed, as Otani grew mellower and more relaxed by the minute, he had to remind himself consciously not to seek out the bare feet he was accustomed to do when dining alone with Hanae, but to keep his own primly tucked out of harm's way for fear of finding the wrong prey.

The jangling of the telephone came as an unwelcome disturbance, but Otani hauled himself away from the pleasant warmth philosophically, since the call was almost certain to be for him. He was far from being fuddled, but he still rubbed a hand over his face as he picked up the receiver. He was unusual among Japanese in identifying himself when answering the phone instead of using the meaningless all-purpose ''*moshi-moshi*'' which merely communicates the information that there is a sentient being at the other end of the line.

''Oh, good, I was hoping you'd be at home. Not interrupting your favourite programme, I hope?'' The voice of the caller was hearty and the language and manner informal to a degree. Otani should have recognised it at once, but was still in the dark until the man spoke again. ''Hello?

Are you there, Superintendent? Atsugi here. Foreign Office Liaison."

"Yes, yes. Of course. Good evening, Ambassador. I didn't recognise you at first. This is an unexpected pleasure."

Atsugi was unruffled by the delicate rebuke. "Look, I'd like a word with you."

"Go ahead."

"No, I mean, in person. I'm not very far away from your place at the moment. Could I persuade you to meet me at Rokko Station in, say, fifteen or twenty minutes?"

Otani was intrigued. He had had a number of confidential conversations with Atsugi, the senior Japanese diplomat assigned to a special liaison office in Osaka to facilitate dealings with the whole Consular Corps of the Osaka–Kobe area, since he had arrived three years earlier. Atsugi was a great improvement on his predecessor, a polite adversary of Otani's who had been dispatched under a cloud to one of the less salubrious republics south of the Sahara.

Atsugi had never previously sought him out in the evening, however; nor made his way to a place conveniently close to Otani's house, as it seemed obvious that he must have done on this occasion. Otani looked at his watch. It was still only eight-fifteen. "Very well," he said. "I can be there in ten minutes."

"Good."

The downstairs phone was in the kitchen, and before returning to the living-room Otani mounted the old wooden staircase to retrieve his jacket from the cupboard in the upstairs room where he knew Hanae would have hung it after relieving him of it on his arrival home earlier. The nights were now very chilly, and he stopped long enough to put on a pullover too.

Then he went downstairs again. "I'm afraid I have to go out for a while," he announced as Hanae looked at him, startled by his changed appearance. "Something has

37

cropped up. Connected with what happened yesterday," he added for Hanae's benefit. He would have said more, but by common consent they had kept Rosie in the dark about what had happened, on the grounds that it would have been too complicated to explain, as well as being hardly a suitable thing to discuss with a foreign visitor. Otani could think of no other reason why Ambassador Atsugi should seek an urgent meeting with him in what amounted to clandestine circumstances.

"I don't suppose I'll be long," he predicted confidently as Hanae came to the front entrance hall to see him off and he was bending to put on his shoes. "An hour or so, probably. I shall look forward to that bath when I get back."

Chapter 5

ATSUGI WAS VERY FAR FROM BEING THE CONVENTIONAL diplomat, even though he was senior enough to have the personal rank of ambassador. His overseas career had been almost wholly in the United States, culminating in several years as Japanese Consul-General in San Francisco, and had left its mark on him. The big man was waiting near the bank of ticket machines at Rokko Station and beamed when he caught sight of Otani entering the approach to the small suburban station. "Want a beer, or shall we take a little stroll?" he boomed while Otani was still some yards away.

Otani opted for the stroll, and Atsugi set a cracking pace up the hill again, in the direction of the campus of Kobe University. After his initial greetings Otani remained silent, waiting for Atsugi to get down to business. It was in any case quite an effort to keep up with him and he had little breath to spare. The diplomat himself made several false starts, apologising again for dragging Otani out of his house, commenting on the contrast between the pleasant warmth of the January sun by day and the crispness of the

39

evenings, and complaining that the very low humidity gave him a tickle in his throat.

Then they had arrived on the hillside campus with its spectacular views over Kobe Port and the whole of Osaka Bay with the Inland Sea beyond, and stopped to take it in. "Look, over there to the left you can see the lights of Wakayama Prefecture," Otani said, panting slightly after the climb. "Well, what's on your mind, Ambassador?"

"I need hardly spell it out, do I? You were there. The Foreign Ministry takes a poor view of attempts on the lives of ambassadors accredited to this country. Even if they don't succeed."

"Yes, I suppose they do. But it's hardly your responsibility, is it? I'm sure the Kyoto police will make a thorough investigation, and no doubt the National Police Agency in Tokyo will be involved. I'm expecting to have to make some kind of statement as a witness—maybe my wife too, but I don't think we can be of any more help than anyone else who was in the room."

Atsugi's rich baritone laugh was infectious, and Otani smiled without quite knowing why. "Come on, now, Superintendent, don't be naive. This case is going to call for quite exceptional handling. In the first place, it's most unlikely that the guy who fired that shot is still in Kyoto Prefecture. The day after tomorrow a whole bunch of European ambassadors, including your British buddy, are due to open some trade fair or other, and having missed his chance yesterday in spite of some fancy shooting our friend may take another pop right in your own backyard."

"Yes. As a matter of fact I've been in touch with both the Kyoto police and the Agency in Tokyo today. There'll be maximum security at the Trade Centre and everywhere the VIPs go, I can assure you." Atsugi laughed again and clapped Otani on the shoulder. With anyone else Otani would have been shocked and outraged by the physical contact.

"My, you don't give out too much unless you have to, do you? It's like pulling teeth talking to you. Sure I know you've been talking to the Agency. So have we."

"So?"

"So what?"

"What have you brought me up here to ask me or to tell me?"

Although there was very little lighting on the quiet university campus, it was very far from being completely dark, and Otani could see Atsugi's face quite clearly. As he waited for him to reply, he once more felt grateful for the straight way the other man had of dealing with him, so different from the Machiavellian deviousness and flowery circumlocutions of his predecessor.

Atsugi turned right round and propped his back against the metal rail on which they had both been leaning to gaze at the spangled lights far below. "Ask, or tell?" he mused. "Both those things. I have to ask you on behalf of the Foreign Ministry to take the lead in co-ordinating the investigation of the shooting in Kyoto yesterday. And I have to tell you that you'll be receiving instructions to that effect from the National Police Agency first thing tomorrow."

Otani's response was as automatic as it was tinged with regret. "Out of the question, Ambassador. I have no jurisdiction or authority in Kyoto Prefecture."

"Not at the moment, I agree. But you'll be given it. Listen to me for a moment, Otani-san. There are political considerations in this case which are perfectly obvious, and it must be handled with great delicacy. We don't want the Kyoto police muddying the waters by haring off into a lot of pointless questioning of the Grand Master's family and people in the tea ceremony organisation when what we're looking for is a terrorist hit-man. Our preliminary investigations suggest that the most likely organisation to be out for the ambassador is an outfit called the Irish Republican Army. It seems they've knocked off at least two British

41

ambassadors in other countries in recent years. I don't need to bother you with the background, but you may know that the British still run a piece of Ireland and there's been trouble there for years. The IRA as they call themselves get a lot of help from the United States—I do believe there are probably more people of Irish background in New York than there are in Dublin.''

Otani had, needless to say, heard of New York but was not too sure about Dublin. In any case he was at that moment much more concerned about the problems looming much nearer home, and shook his head worriedly. "It won't do, Ambassador. Whatever the background may be, the fact of the matter is that the Iemoto was killed. Call it murder, call it accidental death, call it whatever you like, but it happened in Kyoto and the Kyoto police are responsible for investigating it.''

He reached into his jacket pocket and pulled out a packet of Mild Seven cigarettes. He was still half-heartedly trying to give them up, and managing for the most part to smoke only in the open air. He offered the pack to Atsugi, who shook his head and waited in silence until Otani had lit his own and taken a thoughtful puff. "My wife and I were witnesses, and as such will of course co-operate in that investigation. We have to keep it quite separate from measures that need to be taken for the protection of the British Ambassador and the others while they're in Kobe. That *is* my responsibility. But assuming that the opening ceremony passes without incident, then my responsibility ends once they leave Hyogo Prefecture.''

"Come, let's walk a little way more," Atsugi said. "It's chilly standing around.'' They strolled on, past the teaching blocks and towards the main entrance. "I see your point, of course. But look at it from our point of view. The ambassador spends most of his time in Tokyo, right? And of course, the Tokyo Metropolitan Police Special Branch have the job of protecting all the Embassies and their staff routinely. Whenever he leaves Tokyo—and this particular man is a great traveller, I may say—it's up to the police authorities in any prefecture he visits to make sure he comes to no harm. You've already referred to your own responsibility right here . . . but we're not just talking about precautionary measures in general. We've had an actual attempt on his life. Okay, it was unsuccessful, and some other poor guy took the bullet. But you must see that the investigation of what happened in Kyoto yesterday cannot be dissociated from the ambassador's security here and anywhere else he goes. And we don't dictate his movements.''

Otani threw his cigarette down and ground it under his foot. ''Ambassador, let me ask you a question. How do you think I would react if the National Police Agency were to instruct the commander of, say, Okayama Prefectural Police Force to take the lead in the investigation of a killing which took place in the middle of downtown Kobe?''

Atsugi emitted a curious barking sound which Otani concluded must be laughter. ''Maybe I'll get them to try it on you some time, just for the hell of it,'' he said eventually as they made their way down the hill again, this time on the well-lit main road. ''Listen, Otani-san. There was only one real alternative to what they and we decided; and that would be to bring someone down from the National Police Agency to take charge. He would have no local knowledge and would bug everybody around, including yourself and your opposite number in Kyoto. You know how all we Kansai people feel about those slickers from Tokyo.''

It was Otani's turn to laugh, at the quintessentially metropolitan Atsugi's identification of himself with the proudly independent people of the Kyoto–Osaka–Kobe area.

''Anyway,'' Atsugi went on, ''I've already warned you. You'll be getting your formal orders first thing in the morning, and I don't think the Agency will be greatly moved by the idea that the Kyoto man might be put out. We want

43

this man caught, Superintendent. We want him caught before he can get the ambassador. And when you do catch him, we have him on a ready-made charge of murder, don't we?''

Otani stopped short and Atsugi had to walk back two paces to rejoin him. "I won't accept it just as a personal assignment. Let me make that quite clear to the Agency. If I'm to do this I must have full authority to deploy my own staff as I see fit." He glared fiercely up at the much bigger man. "And let me say something else to you personally, Atsugi-san." It was the first time he had broken with convention to address the diplomat by name rather than by rank. "If you already have, or plan to have, any undercover men from the Public Security Investigation Agency operating in my territory, I want to be informed, on a basis of personal confidentiality, if you like. I've suffered altogether too much in the past from interference by the security authorities about which I've been kept in the dark.''

They both started walking again, and had covered quite a long distance before Atsugi spoke again. "Fair enough, Superintendent. I'll keep you in the picture so far as I myself know it." He clapped Otani on the shoulder again. "Right! Now what about that beer?''

Chapter 6

"**I** WAS NOT AWARE THAT I WAS TO HAVE THE PLEASURE of welcoming a delegation," Superintendent Fujiwara almost whispered as the three men entered his office. He had never done anything to discourage the rumour that he was a direct descendant of the great Fujiwaras who had been Ministers, *éminences grises* and de facto rulers of Japan for hundreds of years before the emergence of the Shoguns. In the great days of the Heian Period a thousand years and more ago, Fujiwaras had generally contrived to marry their daughters into the Imperial line, and were from time to time not only fathers-in-law but simultaneously grandfathers and uncles of Emperors both incumbent and retired.

Superintendent Ryo Fujiwara was certainly every inch the aristocrat. His skin was the colour of ivory, his features fine-drawn. If dressed in the Court robes of former centuries, he would have been a perfect model for the notables depicted in the old scroll paintings to be found in every museum. Only his bloodless lips moved as he sat motionless behind a massive desk with a gleaming surface of green leather.

"We are intruding unpardonably," Otani murmured by way of reply, bowing low and suppressing his anger at the discourtesy of their reception. Slightly behind him and to his right, Kimura also bowed, while even Noguchi, spruced up almost unrecognisably in a complete suit, fairly clean shirt and only slightly greasy tie, inclined his head at least three-quarters of an inch.

Fujiwara kept them waiting about ten seconds too long before rising languidly from his chair and bowing perfunctorily. Then he indicated the sofa and armchairs placed for the use of guests and drifted over to them as Otani and his colleagues followed, Noguchi and Kimura reaching into their pockets for name-cards as they did so. After the exchange of cards they all sat down, and Otani presented his best poker face to Fujiwara, who was looking past him with an expression of acute distaste at Noguchi. Noguchi had merely growled incomprehensibly when handing over his card—Kimura even raised an eyebrow in surprise to see that he possessed such things—and now settled into a chair and closed his eyes, effectively removing himself from further contact.

"I am sure," Fujiwara said at last after coughing delicately, "that it has involved you and your, ah, colleagues in considerable inconvenience to make the journey from Kobe for this conference. I am gratified to know that Kyoto has such attractions for you in particular, Superintendent, since you were good enough to come on Sunday also. I trust that Inspector Mihara conveyed my message of welcome to you." His last words were a statement rather than a question, and Otani merely inclined his head by way of reply. In any case, Fujiwara's manner of speech was idiosyncratic to a degree. He paused frequently and some words were spoken so quietly that he seemed in danger of dripping off into elegant slumber in mid-sentence, too weary to continue.

Otani had not come in any expectation of being able to

achieve anything significant by a meeting with Superintendent Fujiwara. He had seen him often enough at conferences of prefectural police commanders in Tokyo, aloof and supercilious, but had never over the years succeeded in having anything like a personal conversation with him. He cleared his throat and sipped at the green tea which had been brought in for all of them by a deferential young policeman. The cup on its fine wooden saucer was of hand-painted delicate china. Expensive, Otani thought, and Fujiwara was studying the design on his own cup with what looked like pleased surprise as he held it in his long, slender fingers.

"It is most unfortunate that the first tea ceremonies of the New Year, normally so auspicious, should have been marred by this distressing affair," Otani said rather bluntly, and Fujiwara blinked at him with a faint smile. Before he could reply, Otani went on. "The reason for my disturbing you today is that I wished to introduce my two senior colleagues to you, Commander. Both will be associated with me in my efforts to collaborate with you and your staff as instructed by the Superintendent-General of the National Police Agency. You have a copy of his telexed order to me, I believe."

A sigh like a summer breeze disturbed Fujiwara's calm for a moment, and Kimura's bright black eyes flickered between the two senior men. It was better than the preliminaries to a bout of *sumo* wrestling. "I have, I have, Superintendent. And of course it is a privilege to receive you. I am quite sure that you will have so much to teach us here in our normally tranquil backwater. Of Inspector Kimura's linguistic talents I have of course heard much." Abruptly his eyes snapped open and his lip curled as he glared at Noguchi, apparently fast asleep. "I have also heard of Inspector Noguchi. I confess myself at a loss to understand what role there may be in this investigation for—" he picked up Noguchi's name-card from the polished table and scrutinised it before tossing it down again "—the head of your Drugs Section."

Noguchi raised one eyelid momentarily and Otani hoped that Fujiwara had seen the glitter as well as he had. "The Inspector's title does not necessarily reflect the scope of his duties," he said, but Fujiwara raised a deprecatory hand and went on imperturbably. "It is of course not for me to comment on such matters, but I am surprised at the absence from this meeting of my old friend and comrade in arms, Inspector Sakamoto of your staff. He is after all, is he not, head of the Criminal Investigation Section of the Hyogo force? It would have been a special pleasure to see him here today."

Otani had not known that Sakamoto was a crony of the head of the Kyoto Prefectural Police. It was a complicating factor, but not one which he proposed to worry about. Nor did he have the smallest intention of involving Sakamoto, whom he detested, in the investigation in more than the most routine context. "Inspector Sakamoto has many duties in Kobe at present, Commander. So indeed have I and my colleagues. We shall therefore not disturb you personally any further, and will I hope be scrupulous to avoid any interference with the work of your officers."

Fujiwara and Kimura each hitched up a trouser leg at precisely the same moment, and Fujiwara shot a glance at Kimura as though uncertain whether or not Kimura was deliberately aping his manner. "You can scarcely hope to do what the Superintendent-General has in his wisdom required you to do without impinging on the proper concerns of my officers," he snapped, the listlessness gone for a moment. "I have instructed Inspector Mihara to act as liaison officer for you. Let me assure you that at least until the British Ambassador leaves Kyoto this afternoon, he will be perfectly safe."

Superintendent Fujiwara uncoiled himself from his chair and seemed to float in the direction of the door where he stood waiting for them to leave. There was a further exchange of bows. "Goodbye, Inspector Noguchi. I have so enjoyed our conversation," Fujiwara murmured as the two inspectors filed out ahead of Otani, who turned in the doorway.

"I am most grateful to you for the friendly spirit of cooperation which has marked this discussion," he said, his face expressionless. "It might have been a difficult, even embarrassing situation for both of us. I now feel much more at ease about what has to be done."

By unspoken consent the three Hyogo men marched out of the building in silence. Otani was not surprised to see Inspector Mihara standing quietly talking to his driver Tomita beside the car in the parking area at the rear. Mihara broke away as soon as he saw Otani and the others and came over to them. "Good morning, Inspector. We've had a . . . useful meeting with Superintendent Fujiwara, who tells me that you have been good enough to agree to assist us."

"My pleasure, sir. Gentlemen." There was a wary look on his face as he saluted the men from Kobe and Otani introduced Kimura and Noguchi.

"There isn't a great deal of time," Otani continued. "We have to step up the security arrangements for the British Ambassador's stay in Kobe, and glean as quickly as possible any relevant considerations from Sunday's shooting incident. I am therefore proposing that my colleagues should go at once to the Southern School headquarters. Inspector Noguchi will examine the exterior of the premises, while I want Inspector Kimura to meet the head of administration—Terada, I believe his name was. Oh, and also the new Grand Master if available. When are the funeral ceremonies planned for?"

"Not until Friday. I think that an interview could be arranged."

"Good. After that I think that if possible Inspector Kimura should travel with the ambassador's party to Kobe. What time are they due to leave?''

''At four-thirty, sir. The ambassador has a meeting with the Governor at the Prefectural Office at four, and then plans to drive straight to the Oriental Hotel in Kobe. We have arranged an escort car with motorcycle outriders all the way.''

''Yes, I meant to report that to you earlier, Chief.'' It was Kimura, looking slightly embarrassed. ''Inspector Mihara and I were talking on the phone first thing, we've sorted everything out with the traffic sections. Our escorts will join the party as they leave the motorway, and take over completely from the moment of arrival at the hotel. The Kyoto motorcycle escorts will turn back at the motorway, of course.''

''All right. It will be dark by the time they get into Kobe City. I want no confusion or security gaps at the hotel, Kimura. Very well. I leave that side of it to the technical experts. Now, Inspector Mihara. If you would be so kind as to contact the tea ceremony people by phone, my colleagues can be on their way.'' He turned to Kimura and Noguchi. ''I'd suggest a taxi. Less conspicuous than going in my car. I shall stay here for a while, then go back to Kobe and wait for you there. I want a few words with Inspector Mihara.''

He felt a momentary pressure against his sleeve and turned to see that Noguchi had strolled off a yard or two, out of immediate earshot. ''Excuse me a moment,'' he said to the others, and went over to his old friend. ''I know what you're going to say, Ninja,'' he began with a smile, but paused when Noguchi shook his head.

''Fujiwara? He's not really upset. Good actor though. I'd say he's worried about something. Bear it in mind. Pal of old Sakamoto, eh? He's probably the one who put that poker up his arse. Just wanted to suggest—see what you can get out of this Mihara. Seems sensible.''

50

It was a rather long speech for Noguchi, and Otani was in a thoughtful mood as he strolled to the road with the others and watched as Kimura hailed a taxi and bounded in, leaving Noguchi to ease his bulk in a more leisurely fashion into the back seat beside him.

Chapter 7

KIMURA WAS ENJOYING HIMSELF. IN THE FIRST PLACE, although he had little knowledge of, or time for, the traditional Japanese ways, he was conscious of the luxuriousness of his surroundings and had looked with satisfaction at the various small gardens, each a gem of artful design, as he passed through the maze of corridors on his way to the office of the administrator, Terada.

Secondly, he was relieved that the office was furnished in the Western style, so that he need not imperil the appearance of his trousers by having to kneel or sit cross-legged on a cushion. The fact that he had as a matter of course been deprived of his shoes on entering the premises and was now wearing a floppy pair of bright green backless plastic slippers did not disturb him: the rule applied universally to Japanese houses, inns and restaurants and was enforced in a surprising number of Western-style buildings too, including schools and even quite a few police stations.

Thirdly, the susceptible Kimura had been delightedly struck by the number of good-looking women about the place. Most were wearing kimonos, but the girl who had brought not tea for once, but coffee into Terada's office for them and must be his secretary was the perfect picture of the highest class of "office lady" in her silk blouse and sleek skirt. Moreover, there had been an awareness in her eye as he caught it which determined him on the spot to make an opportunity to pursue her acquaintance when time permitted.

Finally, Terada had just shown Kimura a list of the names of the senior students at the headquarters school. There were not many of them, and among the Chinese characters in which the names of Japanese are always written, a single entry in the special phonetic script used for foreign names jumped to the eye. It read *"Patoriku Keishii"*.

"I'm surprised that a foreigner would be interested in studying the tea ceremony," Kimura said.

"They write their names back to front, you know," Terada explained helpfully. *"Keishii* is his family name. Rather amusing really, almost the same as the Japanese word for police superintendent." The timid smile on Terada's face faded quickly as Kimura stared at him.

"How is it spelt in Roman letters?"

"Oh. I think I can remember," Terada said, closing his eyes to assist the process. "C-A-S-E-Y, I'm almost sure. The first name is harder. P-A-T-R . . . or maybe L . . . I-K, I think, but I may have missed a letter out. I understand the name is quite common in Ireland where he comes from."

Kimura nodded, trying to suppress the excitement he felt. "I believe it is, yes," he said. "He's a long way from home."

Terada was all eagerness to explain. "Yes. Casey-san is the first real Westerner to study seriously—towards the teaching licence, I mean. Quite a few take lessons, but I fear they tend to lose interest after a while. There have been a number of Japanese-Americans from Hawaii and

53

California who have qualified over the years, but we have high hopes that Casey-san will be the first fully-authorised master of the Southern School to open a branch school in Europe.''

''Indeed. You must be very pleased with his progress. Well, I must get on. Thank you for the list of the guests at the ceremony last Sunday afternoon. And—please forgive me, I have never been present at such a distinguished occasion—I understand from Superintendent Otani who was there that the Grand Master had a number of assistants who distributed cakes or otherwise helped him. Would they have been the people on this list?''

''No. For the New Year ceremonies all the assistants are male, and as you can see, a number of the senior students are women. Masters of branch schools in the Kansai area consider it one of their privileges to assist at the New Year ceremonies, and this is what happened this year as usual. Casey-san was there, however, as a very special privilege. He is about to qualify and receive his teaching licence, and is in any case staying here at present as a guest of the family . . .'' Terada corrected himself. ''I should say, he *was* staying here as a guest. After the tragedy he felt—I must say we were all touched by his thoughtfulness—he felt that he should leave the house to avoid intruding on the family's private grief.''

''I see. Well now, I must not trespass too much on your valuable time, especially when you must have so much to do following the shocking occurrence last Sunday. There are just one or two other points I should like to take up with you, though . . .'' Kimura would have loved to quiz Terada at length about the Irishman Casey, but for reasons best known to himself Otani had laid it down that morning that the strategy in relation to the personnel of the tea ceremony school was to pursue enquiries simply as an investigation into the death of the Grand Master, and to play

54

down the theory that the intention had been to assassinate the British Ambassador.

Kimura therefore asked Terada a number of irrelevant questions about the Grand Master's movements before he entered the room in which he died, the reception system for guests and whether there was any means of identifying them properly. The administrator seemed anxious to cooperate, and replied at somewhat greater length than really suited Kimura, who eventually stared Terada into silence, examined his fingernails, coughed and simulated embarrassment. Then he spoke, with studied hesitations. "Terada-san. Forgive me, but you will appreciate that I am merely carrying out my official duties. I, er, that is . . . I must ask you, are you aware of any enemies the Grand Master might have had? Anyone who might have harboured evil—even murderous—intentions towards him?"

"Such a thing is inconceivable to me." The reply was prompt and almost vehement. "We are all completely at a loss to imagine any possible motive for this terrible crime."

It was precisely what Kimura had expected. "Have you no theory, none at all, about how it might have happened?"

Terada looked a little like a bank manager out of his depth over evidence of a complex fraud involving computers, and shook his head worriedly. "I have racked my brains, Inspector. The only thing I can think is—could it not have been a dreadful accident? It is the hunting season after all, and in the hills to the north of Kyoto we often find hunters and hear gunshots. Someone cleaning a gun in a nearby house, perhaps, and discharging it by mistake?"

Kimura managed to prevent himself smiling as the earnest administrator outlined his preposterous hypothesis, and instead nodded sagely. "It is certainly a possibility which we must look into very carefully, Terada-san. Thank you for your helpful suggestion." He began to stir in his seat. "I have taken far too much of your time, I'm afraid. And

I think you said that the new Grand Master would receive me at eleven-thirty? No, no, please don't trouble yourself, Terada-san. I'm sure your young lady assistant will be kind enough to show me the way.''

It was no use. The young lady in question hovered quite delectably in the vicinity of the door, but Terada was insistent that he must personally effect the introduction to the man who had so suddenly inherited the headship of the school, so Kimura had to content himself with drenching her with one of his most overpowering smiles as he passed. When over a certain age, women generally went a pleasing shade of pink when favoured thus, but Terada's secretary couldn't have been more than twenty-two or -three and looked at Kimura quite coolly, a quizzical twist at the corner of her mouth. The expression was not exactly dismissive, however, and Kimura made a mental note of the fact before turning his mind to the forthcoming interview.

It occurred to him that the family which provided the hereditary heads of the Southern School of the tea ceremony had a pleasingly appropriate name in Minamikuni, or Southern Province. Although Kimura's knowledge of Japanese history was sketchy to say the least of it, he was aware that at one period there were rival Emperors of Japan, one in Kyoto and the other in Yoshino in the mountains of the Kii peninsula, now a couple of hours' ride from Osaka on the private Kintetsu railway. He presumed that the family must have sprung from a favoured courtier of one of the Yoshino Emperors to have been given a name that reverberated so grandly.

Otani had not thought to mention to Kimura that he had seen a photograph of Ko Minamikuni XVIII on the television, and Kimura knew only that the new Grand Master was thirty-two years old. Kimura had recently reconciled himself with some pain to the fact that he was in his early forties—just—and in the process had begun to think of younger men as mere boys. He was therefore unprepared for the vigorous air of authority about the man in Japanese clothing who was waiting for him in the room to which Terada led the way, sliding open a gorgeously-embellished fusuma screen door painted with a background of rich greens and golds and depicting a peacock with tail in full array.

Terada did little more than murmur Kimura's name before standing to one side and then backing out, sliding the door to behind him. It was doubtful whether Otani would have recognised the new Grand Master either, since he could scarcely have resembled less the young man in the photograph on the TV screen. As Kimura approached, his slippers left behind in the wooden-floored corridor, the Grand Master bowed very low from his kneeling position, his forehead almost touching the tatami mat. Kimura hastily knelt and followed suit, not even thinking of his trouser crease until later, and heard a stream of the most elegant expressions of welcome phrased in what to him was the ridiculously affected language of high Kyoto society. Kimura muttered a few conventional phrases of regret in reply, then raised himself cautiously and contemplated the other man.

It was hard to credit that he was only thirty-two. He was in formal black kimono decorated only by the Minamikuni family crest embroidered in the five specified places. The young Grand Master nevertheless looked tough and the hands folded in repose on his lap were big and muscular. The clean-shaven face was somewhat fleshy, and Kimura noticed that his host must patronise a quite fashionable barber, who had left his client's sideburns just a shade longer than would generally be acceptable in conservative society. The only really incongruous note, though, was struck by the tinted glasses the Grand Master was wearing. These did not completely conceal his eyes but made it impossible for Kimura to read their expression. He assumed that the other man must have put them on to hide any puffiness resulting from a combination of grief and exhaustion, but was left with the nagging feeling that the new head of one of the most distinguished families in the country had made himself look a little like a superior gangster.

The preliminaries over, the Grand Master spoke quite directly to Kimura, in a pleasantly cultivated voice. The characteristic Kyoto accent was pronounced, but from then on he avoided the worst extravagances of phraseology. "I understand from Terada-san that you may wish to put some questions to me concerning the death of my father last Sunday. I shall do my best to help you."

Kimura inclined his head in acknowledgement. "You are most kind, *sensei*. I hesitate to trouble you at all at such a time. In fact most of our enquiries can be dealt with quite satisfactorily by members of your staff, and Terada-san has already been very helpful. My main purpose in seeking this brief interview was to assure you that we shall intrude as little as possible into your private distress, but it will of course be necessary for us to examine very carefully the room in which the tragedy took place. One of my colleagues is already at work in the grounds."

"I understand."

Kimura pressed on, still a little unnerved by the unblinking gaze from behind the barrier of the tinted glasses. "Terada-san has already provided me with the relevant information about the guests who were present at the ceremony last Sunday afternoon, and has explained the arrangements so far as the assistants were concerned." Kimura paused for quite a long moment, and the Grand Master helped him out.

"So you want to know where I was at the time," he suggested pleasantly. Kimura nodded. "Not very far away, certainly, but involved with the second stage of the previous ceremony, the first one of the day. It was set for eleven A.M."

Kimura was all at sea, and it must have shown.

"Let me explain what actually happens on these occasions. The waiting period and the actual New Year ceremony takes altogether about an hour or a little longer. Guests are then escorted to another part of the complex here—our new building at the back, actually, where a light meal is served to them and the whole atmosphere is more relaxed and less formal. People don't actually eat very much of the meal—they just taste it and then wrap it up in the *furoshiki* wrapper we provide and take it home." He smiled. "Once the furoshiki were made of real silk. Now they are nylon. There is a kind of lottery too, and two or three lucky guests win souvenir prizes—a fan, or a specimen of calligraphy by my father. It is the custom for my mother, my wife and myself to host this part of the proceedings, moving about among the guests and chatting to them. The meal itself and sake are served by some of our senior students—the ladies, of course. Meantime, guests for the next ceremony are beginning to arrive. We hold three ceremonies on each of two days here in Kyoto, and have a similar programme at our Tokyo branch headquarters the following week."

"Thank you. I apologise for my ignorance." Kimura was genuinely surprised and not a little impressed by the smooth assembly-line arrangements as described by the Grand Master. "There were, therefore, quite a large number of people involved in the proceedings here on Sunday."

"Indeed, yes. At least thirty, I suppose. One moment." Minamikuni's lips moved silently as he counted quickly on his fingers. "No, probably nearer forty, if you include the people outside marshalling cars, the reception staff and so on. Terada-san could probably make a complete list for you fairly easily."

"One last question, if I may, sensei." Kimura found himself using the honorific form of address, "Teacher", quite unself-consciously. "How many people actually *live* on the premises here?"

Again the answer came promptly and openly. "In the private family apartments, my parents. I should say my mother now, of course." Kimura made a solemn face. "My wife and myself, and our son. He's five. There is a maid who lives in, and of course the *banto-san.*"

Japanese inns of the more expensive type commonly employ *banto* or nightwatchmen/porters and after a moment's reflection Kimura realised that one would be needed for premises so full of priceless objects as the historic headquarters of the Southern School.

"I should explain that we are seldom all here at the same time," the Grand Master continued. "Only at New Year, during the *obon* festival in August, and for special family occasions or when receiving particularly important visitors like heads of state or other Government guests when they visit Kyoto. I normally live in my own house elsewhere in Kyoto, with my wife and child, and I also have a flat in Tokyo where I have to spend a lot of time on business."

"I am sorry. I said it was the last question, but I have one more."

"Dozo. Goenryo naku." The Grand Master's go-ahead could not have been more courteous.

"Apart from members of the family and the two servants you mentioned, do you ever accommodate guests overnight here?"

"Oh yes, frequently. An old-fashioned place like this, and as spacious, is very adaptable. There are plenty of tatami floors to sleep on, and we keep stocks of spare bedding. Members of our staff, visiting masters and even senior students quite often spend the night here if we are preparing for a big occasion. That is why I prefer to live in my own house."

He no longer seemed young at all to Kimura as he rocked back slightly on his haunches and surveyed him. "I think
60

I see what you are driving at, Inspector. And I must confirm with regret that these premises are all too accessible to anyone wishing to plan an attempt on the life of a distinguished guest.'' Kimura strained to read the expression in the shaded eyes as the Grand Master continued, but without success. "It is a matter of great shame to this house that His Excellency the British Ambassador was fired upon. We must be thankful that the attempted assassination was unsuccessful, even though it had such tragic consequences for our family.''

In the circumstances, Kimura saw little point in going over the ground he had covered, however perfunctorily, with Terada, and judged in any case that it was time to go. His own lower limbs were completely dead as a result of kneeling on a flat cushion for so long, and he winced as he rose after a final low bow and began to hobble towards the fusuma door, impressed by the smooth ease with which Minamikuni rose to his own feet and seized his elbow to help him.

"It can be painful if one isn't used to it,'' the Grand Master said.

Chapter 8

AS HE TURNED AWAY AFTER MAKING HIS FAREWELLS to Minamikuni, Kimura was pleased and surprised to see Terada's attractive secretary standing quietly at the end of the corridor, apparently waiting for him. Although pins and needles were still racing like darts of ice and fire through his legs, he straightened himself up bravely and tried the smile again. This time it was returned. Not with quite the incandescence which Kimura always tried to achieve when ingratiating himself with a woman, but encouragingly warm all the same.

"Terada-san was called away, I'm afraid. I'll show you the way out."

"How very kind of you. I'm so sorry, I didn't introduce myself to you properly. I am—"

"Inspector Jiro Kimura from Kobe. I know. My name is Mie Nakazato. How do you do."

"Delighted to meet you, Nakazato-san. I wonder—on the way out, would it be possible for me to see the room in—the new extension, I think the Grand Master said. Where the guests have their meal after the tea ceremony?"

"Of course. I expect you'd like to see the room where . . . it happened, too. This way."

Kimura followed at a suitable distance, hanging back a little so that he could admire the way Miss Nakazato's hips swayed as she walked. As a member of the office staff she was spared the green plastic slippers and wore what were obviously her own soft indoor shoes. They fitted her feet snugly and Kimura felt at a disadvantage as he slopped behind. Otani frequently teased Kimura about his marked preference for European or American woman friends but as a matter of fact his mind was far from closed on the subject, particularly in the case of Japanese girls who were taller and better endowed than average. Miss Nakazato struck him as being likely to become more and more interesting on riper acquaintance.

So accurate had been Otani's description of the room in which the tea ceremony had been interrupted that Kimura felt as if he had seen it before. Terada had been unable to provide immediately a plan of the seating arrangement as finally settled by the guests themselves, but had undertaken to try to produce one after consultation with the local tea master who had acted as the principal assistant. The others who had distributed the cakes had been in the room for only a short time and would in any case have been unlikely to recognise all of the guests by sight.

The room in the new extension where the meal was to have been served was a revelation to Kimura. Although the floor was of tatami matting the room itself was airy and light, quite obviously of the late twentieth century and with an atmosphere in sharp contrast to the subdued austerity and almost religious gloom of the other room. "We can serve meals to up to thirty or more people here at a time," Mie Nakazato said with an air of proprietorial pride. "The actual food is supplied by one of the most famous restaurants in Kyoto, but there's a kitchen and servery behind where it can be arranged, and for heating *miso* soup and

63

so on. There's one thing I'd be very interested to know,'' she continued without any change in her manner of speaking. ''Why have you come from Kobe to see us here? Isn't it a matter for the Kyoto police?''

Kimura had been gazing at her intently, trying to decide whether she had had the ''Mongolian fold'' removed from her eyelids by cosmetic surgery as many Japanese girls do, and did not at once take in the question. ''I beg your pardon?''

''I asked why you are concerned with this affair rather than the Kyoto police. I imagine the Grand Master asked you the same thing.''

''No, as a matter of fact he didn't. It's quite coincidental really. The Commander of the Hyogo Prefectural Police Force and his wife happened to be here as guests on Sunday, as you of course know, so they were witnesses. I'm his . . . well, his deputy, more or less. I think the Kyoto police felt it would be simpler if we were to handle things on their behalf.''

Kimura hoped that like most lay people, the toothsome Miss Nakazato would have only a vague idea about police procedures and that his wholly unconvincing explanation of his involvement might satisfy her. He was disappointed.

''I see,'' she said, manifestly sceptical. ''I thought it might have something to do with the British Ambassador. I saw in the paper this morning that he's supposed to go to Kobe later this week to open a trade fair. And he and his wife were here on Sunday, of course.''

Kimura nodded and made an airy gesture with one hand which just happened to brush the girl's shoulder through the silk of her blouse; at which Kimura apologised profusely. The warmth of her skin was quite delightful. ''Yes, another odd coincidence,'' he said then. ''Very distressing for the ambassador, I'm sure. He's to visit Kobe, is he? I do remember reading something about a trade fair, but that sort of thing hardly concerns us in the police, you know.

64

Except for the traffic department, of course." Kimura gave a merry, dismissive little chuckle which died on his lips as he saw Miss Nakazato's expression become one of polite disbelief.

"That's rather strange," she said with careful courtesy. "I have a message for you from the Governor's office. The British Ambassador will be expecting you there following his meeting with the Governor and would be pleased if you would ride with him and his wife to Kobe in their car."

Kimura thought fast, and cleared his throat in an official manner, drawing himself up rather stiffly. "It would have been helpful if you had passed on that message at once, rather than waiting till now, Nakazato-san. It concerns confidential police business, you see."

The girl seemed to be taken aback by Kimura's sudden change of manner and the eclipsing of his earlier radiance towards her, and looked down in some confusion.

Kimura waited until she raised her head again, and then adjusted his features so as to project what he hoped looked like stern kindliness. "Nakazato-san," he asked, "how long have you worked here at the Southern School headquarters?"

Mie Nakazato was rapidly regaining her poise, and there was a hint of impishness in her brown, intelligent eyes. "Nearly two years."

"As Terada-san's secretary throughout that time?"

"Yes."

Kimura took a deep breath, and risked a twinkle. "I should like to ask a favour of you. In return I will confirm that we cannot completely rule out the possibility that what happened here last Sunday might have a bearing on the British Ambassador's personal security. That is why I shall be travelling down to Kobe with him this afternoon." Miss Nakazato nodded slightly in acknowledgement. "The favour I ask is this. Please do not mention this to any of your colleagues. May I have your assurance on that point?"

She nodded again. "I won't say anything."

"Did you take the call from the Governor's office yourself?"

"Yes."

Kimura was relieved. He knew perfectly well that there was no effective way of maintaining confidentiality about their involvement nor about their concern for the ambassador's security. Otani's instructions were simply to play it down so far as possible. If he could also induce Mie Nakazato to see herself in a slightly conspiratorial relationship to himself, he might well be able to pick up some useful additional information about Patrick Casey: not to mention the distinct likelihood of his being able to get to know her better. Much better.

Kimura smiled at her, careful to aim at merely friendly rapport. "Good, that's agreed, then." He took a last look round the spacious, luxurious room, then moved towards the corridor through the glass windows of which the bamboo grove was partially visible. The sight reminded him of Noguchi, and he turned to Miss Nakazato. "I must have a word with my colleague. I expect he's still outside." As he spoke, it occurred to Kimura that even if Noguchi had wanted to come in it was most unlikely that he would have been willingly admitted to such classy premises, suit and tie notwithstanding. "After that I wonder if I could persuade you to have some lunch with me nearby? There are some questions I should like to ask you in strict confidence."

Miss Nakazato looked startled and more than a little suspicious as she considered the invitation, but only hesitated for a moment. "I normally eat lunch here . . . but since Terada-san won't be back before mid-afternoon I suppose I . . ."

"Good," Kimura said briskly, and looked at his watch. He was dogged by ill-luck in the matter of timepieces, and his latest electronic purchase was behaving erratically. "Yes, it's more or less lunchtime," he surmised. "I'll be waiting for you outside the front gate in about fifteen minutes.''

''All right. Just after twelve-thirty,'' the girl agreed after a glance at her own watch, and led him round the corridors to the main entrance where his shoes were neatly positioned on the stone floor below the wooden step, a long-handled shoehorn conveniently to hand so that he could step into them. Kimura made his way round to the side of the main building, on stepping stones set into the white gravel, and looked hopefully in the direction of the bamboos.

''You took your time,'' Noguchi said, materialising at his side from behind, and Kimura jumped.

''I didn't see you, Ninja,'' he said irritatedly, by no means for the first time in his career.

''Saw you, though, didn't I? Found a new girlfriend, I see.''

''Whatever do you mean, Ninja?'' Kimura coloured slightly. If Noguchi had added the ability to see through solid walls to his other talents life would become impossible.

''I was under the floor if you want to know. Heard every word.''

Kimura studied his colleague. The tie had disappeared, presumably stuffed into a pocket of the jacket which had also been removed; and from Noguchi's begrimed appearance Kimura could well believe that he had been crawling about in the open space underneath the wooden structure of the buildings.

Noguchi gazed blandly back. ''Mustn't keep you from your lunch date. Thought you might like to see this, though.'' Noguchi rummaged in his trouser pocket and produced a small plastic bag which he handed to Kimura. Inside it was a brass bullet-case.

''Where—''

''In the bamboos. Very careless of him.'' Noguchi took

his trophy back before Kimura had scarcely had time to do more than glance at it, sniffed, and wiped his nose with the back of his beefy hand. Although his craggy, battered features rarely revealed his state of mind, Kimura inferred without difficulty that his colleague was feeling pleased with himself.

"I'll be off back to Kobe, then," Noguchi said. "Leave you to your new playmate." He half turned away then changed his mind. "Fujiwara," he said. "Put me in mind of you a bit."

Kimura was outraged. He had tried to draw Noguchi out on the subject of the commander of the Kyoto force while in the taxi on the way to the Minamikuni headquarters, without success. "Now come *on*, Ninja. A joke's a joke, but . . ."

"You think at first that he's all piss and wind, then you realise he might be smarter than he acts." While Kimura was taking this in, Noguchi suddenly clapped him on the back, nearly knocking the breath out of him. "Watch it, though. Seems he's a pal of Sakamoto."

Then Noguchi was gone, and Kimura slipped his jacket off and brushed the back fastidiously with a paper handkerchief before putting it back on and straightening his tie in preparation for his rendezvous with Mie Nakazato. One never knew what Noguchi had been handling, but could be reasonably confident that it would have been something not very nice.

Chapter 9

"**Y**ES, INSPECTOR. DO COME IN. WHAT CAN I DO FOR you?" Otani's manner was mild and courteous, even though the last thing he wanted was a discussion with the head of the Criminal Investigation Section, who had rapped on his office door within five minutes of Otani's return to Kobe. "I must be rather brief, I'm afraid: I have a busy afternoon ahead of me."

Inspector Masao Sakamoto marched in, halted and stood rigidly to attention two yards in front of Otani's desk, his lips pursed disapprovingly and his thin features tense. In spite of the nature of his duties, Sakamoto usually wore uniform about headquarters, and Otani noted the perfection of his turn-out, even though as usual his collar seemed a size or two too big for him, so that the scrawny neck moved when he turned his head, while the shirt itself remained motionless. The skin of his face and head seemed on the other hand to be drawn more tightly over the bones of his skull than is the case with most people, making his eyes protrude.

"I wish to lodge a formal complaint, Commander," he announced in his vinegary voice.

69

"Oh? I am sorry to hear that. What is it . . . this time?" Sakamoto seldom sought an interview with Otani unless to lodge a complaint, and Otani rarely himself found occasion to summon him. Guessing what was coming, Otani fixed his gaze on Sakamoto's prominent Adam's apple which wobbled disconcertingly as he spoke.

"I am informed that you were this morning in conference with Superintendent Fujiwara of the Kyoto Prefectural Police, sir."

Otani nodded. "That is so. From time to time I have occasion to make contact with my opposite numbers in neighbouring prefectures."

"Inspectors Noguchi and Kimura accompanied you to Kyoto."

"Your information is quite correct, Inspector Sakamoto." The Adam's apple lurched up and down before Sakamoto spoke again. "May I ask why I was excluded, Commander?"

"By all means. Your presence was not required, Inspector." Otani let the silence draw itself out, half expecting Sakamoto to turn on his heel and leave the room. He even reached for some of the papers which had been placed on his desk during his absence, but put them down again when he heard a kind of strangulated cough.

"Commander, I should like to inform you that Superintendent Fujiwara is a very old personal friend of mine."

"Yes. So I believe. In fact, the Superintendent mentioned it to me this morning. You served together during the war, I understand."

With an inward sigh Otani prepared himself for a longer and more trying conversation than might normally have been expected. Kimura had occasionally speculated to Otani over a beer about Sakamoto's wartime career. He had a theory that Sakamoto had either been a bloodthirsty sword-wielding *bushido* type, or more likely an NCO in the catering corps who had been over-compensating ever since.

70

Otani himself had never bothered to call for his confidential personnel file, but now made a mental note to do so, if only for the light it might throw on Fujiwara's background.

"Superintendent Fujiwara telephoned me on a personal basis after your discussion to express surprise at my absence. In view of the fact that the Hyogo force has been given the responsibility for investigating the death by shooting of the Iemoto of the Southern School—"

"Not the Hyogo force, Inspector. The assignment is a personal one, to me."

"However that may be, sir, it seems that you have already called upon the assistance of two senior officers, neither of whom is properly responsible in any way for criminal investigation duties, although I am very well aware that you habitually employ them outside their proper spheres."

Not for the first time, Otani felt a pang of guilt with regard to Sakamoto. He stood up, and moved round the edge of his desk. "Come, Inspector," he said. "Shall we sit down for a moment?" He led the way to the easy chairs, sat down and watched Sakamoto perch himself stiffly on the edge of the chair opposite. "You are annoyed, and with some justification. I should like to speak very frankly, therefore." Sakamoto stared fixedly over Otani's shoulder, making no reply.

"As head of this force, I reserve the right to take personal charge of any case within our jurisdiction, and to call upon any officer to assist me in any way I judge expedient. It is a matter of regret to me that you are not on good personal terms with Inspector Noguchi, nor with Inspector Kimura. I depend heavily on the special skills of those two officers."

"You may depend on mine also, sir. But you do not choose to do so."

"Hear me out, please, Inspector. I was referring to our normal duties. The present case is unusual. It is also deli-

71

cate. I have, as I already explained, been assigned on a personal basis to look into it, and I have selected your two colleagues to help me in the preliminary stages. I may well seek your assistance also. It would encourage me to do so if I felt that you could work with the others in a friendly spirit of cooperation, rather than one of jealous possessiveness over areas of responsibility."

Something seemed to snap in Sakamoto, and his straight back slumped slightly. "Perhaps that is how it seems to you. But you do me injustice, Superintendent." Otani sat back, uneasily aware that Sakamoto had never to his knowledge trespassed into the preserves of either Kimura or Noguchi, but doggedly gone about his proper business, unimaginatively perhaps but not without efficiency. Sakamoto went on. "It is common knowledge in this headquarters that you dislike me and exclude me from your confidence. I for my part have tried to serve you loyally and to the best of my ability. However, you prefer to work with a conceited tailor's dummy like Kimura and a disgusting, unwashed animal like Noguchi."

Otani raised an eyebrow but let Sakamoto have his head. It was the first time he had ever known him to lose control of his tongue, and the thaw in his habitual wintry formality was almost appealing.

Sakamoto licked his thin lips with a dry, leathery lizard tongue then took out a paper handkerchief and dabbed at his forehead. "I have no alternative but to request a transfer, sir. I'm putting in a formal application today. Superintendent Fujiwara has said that he would welcome me to the Kyoto force. Then you won't have me around to irritate you any longer."

Sakamoto sat well back in his chair for the first time, took a deep breath and subsided. He looked tired, and more human than Otani could remember having seen him before.

"I see," Otani said, then paused before continuing. "Thank you for your frankness with me. I owe you an

72

apology, Inspector, a sincere apology. I have underrated you, and I have been guilty of insensitivity towards you. I shall not stand in the way of your desire to be transferred to the Kyoto Prefectural Police, particularly as you tell me Superintendent Fujiwara has indicated that he will support your application. I'm sure you realise, though, that it will probably take several months for the necessary approval to be obtained from the National Police Agency.'' Otani looked hard at Sakamoto, unable to tell whether he was relieved or dejected now that matters had reached a crisis and that the crisis seemed to have been surmounted.

Then Sakamoto sat up straight again. ''Thank you for agreeing to my request. I think it would be better if the move could take place as soon as possible, sir. Would you see any objection to my being seconded to the Kyoto force on a temporary basis pending formal approval of my transfer? You have the authority to arrange such a secondment by agreement with the other prefectural commander concerned.''

Otani had a fundamental objection to being rushed or pressurised, and sucked in his breath dubiously. ''I don't see any great urgency about the matter,'' he said at length. ''After all, you'll need to look into the question of accommodation, and other personal . . .''

''I think it would be better to make a clean break, sir. I could clear my desk today and report to Kyoto tomorrow morning without any difficulty.''

''Is that so? You really are in a hurry, aren't you? And who is to take over your duties here, may I ask?'' Sakamoto did not even attempt to answer the question, and after a moment Otani made a little gesture of acceptance. ''Very well, Inspector. If you are so keen to be gone, it would be better for me not to obstruct you.'' He stood up and extended a hand to Sakamoto. ''It's your decision, Inspector. I wish you well in your new work . . . and I thank you for the service you have rendered to the Hyogo force. I presume you have already cleared this secondment business with Superintendent Fujiwara?'' Sakamoto nodded as they briefly shook hands. Otani could not for the life of him imagine why he had made such an alien gesture, and relinquished Sakamoto's dry, bony palm hurriedly. Then the two men bowed, and Sakamoto began to move to the door.

"As senior headquarters duty officer yesterday and today I can confirm that all the necessary security arrangements for the arrival of the British Ambassador and for his stay in Kobe have been made, sir.''

"Thank you. I am sure they have. Goodbye, Inspector, and good luck.'' Otani held the door open, nodded once more at the departing Sakamoto, then closed it after him and returned to his desk. Knowing Sakamoto's work methods, he was quite sure that all the necessary paperwork associated with his transfer and immediate prior secondment to the Kyoto force would be prepared impeccably before the end of the afternoon. He was, however, still slightly shaken by Sakamoto's explosive and, for him, highly uncharacteristic outburst, and sat pondering for a while before being disturbed by the sound of the door opening again. It was Noguchi, who never knocked before entering, and now shuffled in and made for his usual chair.

"Ah, Ninja, you're back. Good. Pity you weren't here a little earlier—you'd have heard some home truths about yourself.'' Otani went to join him and smiled as Noguchi opened one eye in what for him was an extravagant display of surprise. "Sakamoto. He doesn't like you. He thinks you're a—oh, never mind.''

"What's he on about now?''

"He's leaving us, Ninja.'' Noguchi opened the other eye. "He was more or less lying in wait for me when I got back here. Began by complaining about being kept out of this morning's meeting in Kyoto, and then went on to a generalised complaint about the way I treat him.'' Otani sighed, and reached for a cigarette. In spite of his resolution about not smoking indoors, he felt he needed one. "Not wholly unjustified, Ninja." He patted his pockets, trying to find his lighter, and Noguchi reached a hand into his own jacket pocket and produced a box of matches which he passed to Otani. The box bore the name and telephone number of a very expensive bar, and Otani registered the fact with some surprise.

"Anyway," he continued, "he then went on to make a formal request for transfer, and while it's going through, asked me to agree to his immediate secondment. Effective tomorrow." Otani would not have been so open in discussing Sakamoto's abrupt departure with any of his colleagues other than Noguchi.

"Where's he want to go?"

"Kyoto. You heard Fujiwara say he's a friend of his."

Noguchi slowly hauled himself into an upright position in his chair. "And you agreed?"

"Of course I did. I can't keep the man here against his will. At least I could for a while, I suppose, but what would be the point? He never has fitted in, you don't like him, nor does Kimura . . . and nor do I, quite frankly."

Noguchi's hand rasped over his stubbly chin. "I don't like it."

"Why not?" Otani thought he knew the answer to his own question as he asked it, but wanted time to think.

"Obvious, isn't it? Fujiwara wanted Sakamoto in on this case once he knew the Agency was putting you on to it. Why? Not just because they're old pals. What are friends for? Why does Sakamoto suddenly take it into his head to get a transfer? Could have done it years ago if he felt that way." Noguchi glared at Otani. "Want my advice? Stall him. Hold up the papers. Unless you want Sakamoto getting underfoot while you're sorting out the Kyoto end of the Minamikuni killing. Keep him down here till you've finished. Then get rid of him fast as you like."

Otani had been drawing deeply on his cigarette as Noguchi spoke, and now leaned forward and stubbed it out, half-finished. "No, Ninja. I see your point, of course. And perhaps I was wrong to agree to the secondment. But I've done it now, and I'm not going back on my word." He flung himself back in his chair, his mind racing. The implications of Noguchi's words were disturbing, and Otani recalled his old associate's warning as they had parted after the curious meeting in Fujiwara's office.

"If he does get in our way in Kyoto we shall at least be forewarned, thanks to you, Ninja. But what on earth could Fujiwara be up to? I can understand his being upset, but why he should want Sakamoto there with him I can't imagine. I wonder what job he'll give him?"

"Soon find out, won't you? By the way, I found the shell-case."

"What?" Otani's thoughts were far away.

"The shell-case. From the bullet that killed Minamikuni. Forensic have got it. I found it among the bamboos, not far from the wall. Couldn't have been there more than a couple of days. Can't be many knocking around those grounds. Must be the one."

"Really? You found it? Splendid! Anything else of interest?"

Noguchi grunted. "Quite enough for one day, I should have thought. Kimura got off with some bird in the office there. Bright kid. Knew what we were really up to, but Kimura handled her all right." Noguchi eased himself forward, in preparation for the protracted business of getting up out of his chair. "Well. I'll be getting along. Putting the word out among some of my grasses. If there's a visiting professional gun in town I'll let you know."

Otani nodded, and watched as Noguchi made for the door. "Good. Thank you, Ninja. Oh, Ninja!" Noguchi turned slowly. "Have you got any contacts in Kyoto?"

A sardonic smile flickered briefly over the battered features. "What do you think? Lot of Koreans in Kyoto.

Plenty of *burakumin*." Noguchi's intimate Korean connections had once been unknown and were still confidential to Otani and only a very few others. On the other hand, most of the headquarters staff knew how effectively Noguchi exploited his contacts among the hereditary outcast groups, historically the leather-workers, butchers, scavengers and buriers of the dead, and, in spite of post-war legal reforms, still effectively condemned to exclusion from general society and from access to any but lowly occupations.

"You might try to find out if any of the Kyoto gangsters know anything about a contract, as well. This was a refined set-up though. Almost certainly a stranger, and very probably a foreigner, of course. Oh, and while you're about it, I'd be interested to know what your Kyoto contacts think of Fujiwara."

Chapter 10

"**A**ND WHERE DID YOU STUDY ENGLISH, MR KIMU-ra?" Lady Hurtling enquired politely as the Rolls-Royce sped along the Nagoya–Kobe expressway, the Union Jack on its stubby chromium staff on the offside front wing fluttering tautly in the wind.

"Here and there, ma'am," Kimura said, sitting sideways in his blue leather seat next to the driver so that he could survey the VIP couple in the back.

Sir Rodney Hurtling was staring crossly out of the window at the Suntory whisky distillery nestling in the wooded hills to their right, put out by the fact that after listening to a few sentences of his voluble but turbulent Japanese, Kimura had replied in relaxed and idiomatic English which had gratified Lady Hurtling. Kimura for his part was enjoying himself hugely. He had never actually ridden in a Rolls-Royce before, and, though disappointed by the surprisingly restricted size of its interior, was delighted with the luxury of its appointments and by the smooth acceleration of the massive car, rendered even heavier as it was by what Kimura guessed to be complete bullet-proofing.

78

The lunch with Mie Nakazato, in a Western-style steak house not far from the Heian Shrine, had also gone well. The place had been practically deserted, since although the area was dense with school sightseeing groups, the well-heeled foreign tourists who normally patronised such eating-places were absent at that time of the year. Miss Nakazato had seemed suitably impressed by Kimura's show of easy authority as he ordered for them both and persuaded her to drink the glass of red Mercian Brand wine which came with the set lunch.

Now he was busily engaged in charming Lady Hurtling. "We have a great many Westerners living in the Kobe area, and my work brings me into a lot of contact with them. It's really essential in my job to have pretty good English. I studied in Europe—oh dear, more years ago than I care to think about," he added with a boyish laugh to make it plain that he didn't consider himself to be all *that* old. "May I ask if you happen to have any Welsh blood, Lady Hurtling? I spent some time in Wales, and you have that beautiful colouring I noticed in many Welsh girls."

Lady Hurtling gave him an arch little tap on the elbow. "Goodness, what a thing to say, Mr Kimura! Well, as a matter of fact, my family *does* have some Welsh connections." She turned to her husband, who had now turned his head to glower at Kimura. "Isn't that clever of Mr Kimura, Roddy? Fancy his being able to guess! I feel quite flattered." This was transparently obvious to both Kimura and her husband, and the British Ambassador cleared his throat and changed the subject.

"Yes. Well, be that as it may, dear, I must discuss a few points with the Inspector." He paused, torn between languages, since if he were to insist on using Japanese in order to exclude his wife, the driver would understand everything he said; whereas if they used English, Thelma might well intervene. Then again, he had never, in spite of some discreet enquiries which had been instituted on his behalf by those responsible for the Embassy's internal security, been able to discover whether or not his personal driver understood more than a few words of English. Indecisive, he began in Japanese, then switched to English in some desperation when he saw Kimura's expression of polite long-suffering.

"Inspector. I invited you to ride with us in my car—oh hang it, I think I'll use English. Look, I'd like you to satisfy me that there'll be nothing too obtrusive about the security arrangements in Kobe. Mind you, I appreciate that it's a difficult decision for the police, especially after what happened on Sunday. I must say I never thought that if and when it did come it would be in circumstances like that, did you, Thelma?"

Thus appealed to, Lady Hurtling twittered helplessly for a moment, and had just begun to speak coherently when her husband interrupted, ignoring her so that she soon subsided again.

"One rather tended to discount the letters, you see, Inspector. Of course, I reported them, or that is to say one of my staff did so for me, we have regular contact with the Metropolitan Police people needless to say, and the Kojimachi Police Station just round the corner from the Embassy take excellent care of us, I must say . . ."

Kimura took it in in fascination, wondering whether the ambassador would forget to draw breath; but eventually he paused. "Letters, Your Excellency? What letters?"

"Oh, I thought you'd have been told about them. No need to call me Excellency by the way. Sir will do. Nothing necessarily excellent about an ambassador, I always say." Sir Rodney Hurtling barked in brief mirthless laughter and then pressed on. "Letters. Yes, well, just illiterate scrawls, really, weren't they, Thelma? Posted in the Marunouchi district. IRA death threats, but I have my doubts, personally. You'd be surprised if you could see some of the letters that come to me, Inspector. Remember that dog

80

business, Thelma? I began to wonder if the entire population of Japan had taken leave of their senses after the local press picked up that *Daily Mirror* thing about the Japanese ill-treating their dogs. Mind you, they do, if I may say so with all respect. And I told my correspondents so quite frankly, I may say.''

Kimura coughed and the ambassador looked at him sharply.

"Did you say something, Inspector?''

"I was just going to ask—sir—how long ago these death threats were received at the Embassy.''

"I've just been telling you. There were three. It was three, wasn't it, dear? Over a period of about a month. When was the last one, Thelma?''

Again Lady Hurtling opened her mouth to speak but was swept aside by the relentless staccato monologue of the ambassador.

"Must have been about three weeks ago. I remember, I had the Clean Government Party Diet members to a stag lunch that day, just before everything packed up for the holidays. It was very irritating, only three of the eight I'd asked actually came. I don't see how they could all be tied up with year-end parties in the middle of December, do you? I'm sure I don't know how this legend about the Japanese being workaholics arose. Good Lord, I had our junior Industry Minister to cope with the following week even though I keep telling them in London that this endless stream of Ministers and mandarins from Whitehall coming to Japan is counter-productive and that if they'd only *read* my despatches they could save themselves a lot of trouble, not to mention the taxpayers' money. Anyway I don't think my wife and I managed more than a couple of days to ourselves over the entire Christmas period, and then there was the Twelfth Night party to get ready for . . . Thelma!''
He paused with such portentousness that she actually had time to respond.

"Yes, Roddy?"

"Remind me to talk to Oliver about that singularly taste-less skit the Commercial Section put on last week. One is all in favour of a certain amount of good-humoured teas-ing, but that hardly justifies representing me as a pompous bore."

They had passed the Osaka interchanges and in another twenty minutes or so would be leaving the motorway at the point where motorcycle police from the Hyogo force would be waiting to take over from their Kyoto counterparts to escort the ambassadorial Rolls to the centre of Kobe and the Oriental Hotel.

Determined to make the most of the time remaining to him, Kimura raised his voice somewhat. "Roughly be-tween mid-November and mid-December last, then, Am-bassador. And have there been any actual attempts before last Sunday?"

"Attempts? What attempts?" Again Lady Hurtling man-aged to get a word in edgeways. "There was the petrol bomb at the Consular Section, wasn't there, Roddy?"

"Oh really, Thelma, I hardly think that constituted a *bomb*. Now I see what the Inspector was getting at. You didn't make yourself very clear, you know," he added, glasses flashing intimidatingly. "You mean attempts. On my life."

"And mine." Kimura heard Lady Hurtling's subdued contribution, but doubted if her husband had.

"Let me think, now. No. As my wife points out, there was a very incompetent attempt to set fire to our consular offices a couple of months ago. Someone set a small fire in the early hours with the aid of a bottle of petrol outside the main door, but it was a trivial affair and caused negli-gible damage. Hardly IRA style, I'd say, Inspector. My private opinion is that it was some disgruntled Brit with a grievance, like that chap in Bangkok years ago, you re-member, Thelma, the bigamist with the wooden leg." Sir

82

Rodney chortled, this time with an appearance of genuine merriment, and Kimura seized the opportunity to put in another question.

"I presume that the threatening letters you mentioned were handed over to the police in Tokyo, sir? Or at least photocopies of them?"

"Oh, I really couldn't say, my dear fellow. I shouldn't be surprised."

"But you saw them, sir. They did seem to you to be the work of a foreigner—I'm sorry, I mean a native English speaker, rather than a Japanese?"

For the first time the ambassador seemed actually to try to think about what was said to him, rather than dashing off on a tangent. "I took it for granted, really," he said after a while. "Can't remember the exact wording, but one of them at least seemed to indicate a detailed knowledge of place names and particular incidents in Northern Ireland, as I recall."

"We're nearly at the interchange, sir. One last question, if I may. Do you know of many Irish people living in Japan?"

"There's no need for you to change to the Kobe escort car, you know, Inspector Kinoshita."

"*Kimura*, dear. Inspector *Kimura*. You're *awful* with names." Lady Hurtling sounded positively annoyed.

"Kimura. Terribly sorry. All I meant to say was, we can go on chatting as far as the hotel, by all means. Irish in Japan? I haven't the slightest idea really. A few dozen at most, I should think. But whoever fired that gun on Sunday might not necessarily be Irish, you know. From Ireland, I mean. Good Lord, there are hordes of Irish in Liverpool, London and all over the place. Not to mention America. Why the American authorities don't take action, I can't imagine. I find their attitude pusillanimous in the extreme, but then with a man with a name like Reagan in charge and another called Kennedy after the job what can you expect? Not that Kennedy will ever have a chance in my opinion after that shady business with the girl in the car, and his elder brother seems to have been a man of inordinate . . . well, you know what I mean, Inspector, you're a man of the world . . ."

The ambassador was well away, and Kimura kept him going effortlessly for the rest of the drive, merely by putting in the odd word now and then.

Chapter 11

"Hello?"

"*Moshi-moshi!* Is that you, Atsugi-san?" Momentarily put off by the English word, Otani wondered if he had misdialled on his private line and failed to reach the Foreign Ministry man in Osaka.

"*Hai.* Atsugi here. Who's speaking?"

"Otani, Hyogo police. I thought you might have left, or that I'd got the wrong number when you answered in English."

"Sorry, Otani-san, old habits die hard. What can I do for you?"

Otani settled back in his chair and held the phone more comfortably, idly tracing a complex series of triangles on a Ministry of Justice circular with the point of his letter-opener as he talked. He was very fond of that letter-opener, which was fashioned in the shape of a miniature samurai sword, complete with its scabbard and beautiful braided purple silk sling.

"Just one thing, but I'll come to that. We now have the British Ambassador safely installed at the Oriental Hotel

85

here, and I thought you might like to know that Superintendent Fujiwara of the Kyoto prefectural force is every bit as annoyed as I told you he would be. It's been a fairly productive day, though, on the whole. I shall be better pleased when we get this opening ceremony business over tomorrow. We have altogether too many ambassadors to protect for my liking.''

Otani distinctly heard Atsugi's baritone chuckle over the line from his office twenty-five miles distant. "Come now, it's no very big deal, Superintendent. There are many occasions when a dozen or more all attend the same function in Tokyo. And what about the Emperor's Birthday, when every one of them goes off to the Palace to pay his respects? It's not like you to over-react.''

Otani added a little flag to the tracing of the triangles, then pushed the paper away from him. "It was you who got excited about the business on Sunday,'' he pointed out. "Supposing our friend with the rifle has another try at the Trade Centre and misses again? He might get the Governor or the Mayor next time, and then I'd really be in trouble.''

"Well, we shall just have to hope for the best, won't we? How did things go in Kyoto, though? Really.''

Otani was quite glad of the opportunity to marshal his own thoughts by talking to Atsugi. "A little progress, I suppose. I took my two senior colleagues, Noguchi and Kimura, with me to call on Fujiwara. You've met them both, I think.''

"Well, let's say that I know *about* them both, shall we?''

"Quite. Well, as I've already told you, Fujiwara was very cool indeed. I can't say I blame him in the least, even though I must admit he irritated me.''

"I dare say he did. High and mighty, I expect. You know his family background, I take it?''

"I know the rumours. Anyway I was with him for only ten or fifteen minutes. I did my duty in making the courtesy call, but I don't expect to have any further contact with him. There's an inspector there who's liaising with me and I'm finding him extremely helpful. A complete contrast, in fact.''

"Good. So, what have you learned?''

A smile flickered over Otani's face as he shifted his position and stared unseeingly at the gloomy old oil painting which hung on his office wall, put there presumably decades before by one of his predecessors. It was only when he and his principal lieutenants were at a loss for inspiration that they looked properly at the picture and speculated in a desultory way about it.

"Well, Noguchi found the case of what was almost certainly the bullet which killed the Iemoto. We shall know for sure tomorrow when we get the report after the lab has compared it with the slug they took out of his head. Not that we're likely to stumble on the rifle, so it might not be of all that much help. All the same, it's a lead.''

"It is indeed. So? You said there was something I could do for you.''

"Yes. Inspector Kimura has been telling me about the IRA death threat letters to the British Ambassador.''

"Really? How did he find out about them?''

"Sir Rodney Hurtling told him all about them on the way here this afternoon—Kimura was in the car with him and his wife. Said the ambassador hardly stopped talking all the way. Of course you mentioned the IRA to me last night anyway . . . but not the letters.'' Otani let the silence hang between them for a moment before continuing. "The point I'm leading up to is that there was an Irishman staying with the Iemoto's family until Sunday, and he moved out after the killing.''

Otani distinctly heard Atsugi's intake of breath. "I thought you'd be interested. He's been studying the tea ceremony very seriously, it seems, to the point where he's about to receive a teacher's licence. It may be pure coincidence, but I'd like you to have a word with your people and pass me anything they have on a man called Casey. Patrick Casey.'' Otani did his best to pronounce the name in the way Kimura had done, and Atsugi seemed to grasp it. ''I could put in a request through the National Police Agency, but I expect you could get a quicker response.''

''I expect I could, Superintendent. My, you have been working hard. I presume you've already checked him out with immigration records?''

''Of course. And with the Alien Registration Section in the local ward office in Kyoto, of course. His papers seem to be quite in order, and there's no mystery about where he's gone. He checked in in the proper way at a low-budget hotel used mostly by foreigners in the northeast of the city. Not far from the Temple of the Silver Pavilion.''

''Plenty of time to get from there to Kobe for breakfast, shoot Sir Rodney and be back in Kyoto for an afternoon's sightseeing before dinner, all the same.''

''No, no. You misunderstand me. There's no question of Casey having fired the gun on Sunday.'' Otani found himself becoming irritable. ''He was assisting at the tea ceremony. But I suppose he could conceivably have been an accomplice. On the other hand, he has been in Japan on a cultural visa for two years or more, and may well be exactly what he claims to be. All I want to know is whether this man has been in any way an object of interest to the Public Security Investigation Agency in Tokyo. Urgently.''

''Right. I'll get on to it right away and call you back. It's after six now. Are you on your way home?''

Otani looked at his watch. ''I'll be here till seven.''

''Okay. By the way, are you free for lunch tomorrow? It's the Osaka Rotary Club's regular meeting. I know you

88

like to get over here and mingle with the top men once in a while.'' Otani was tempted, in spite of Atsugi's good-natured taunt. It was quite true that the Osaka club boasted some very important members indeed compared with his own Kobe South club, highly respectable though that of course was, but it was impossible for him to get away.

"Not this week, I'm afraid, Ambassador. I mustn't leave Kobe tomorrow. Later in the month, perhaps.'' He rang off and set to work to deal with the routine papers which had accumulated on his desk, hardly expecting Atsugi to call back before he left, but waiting until seven-fifteen anyway. Otani had already notified his driver that he would go home on the train, and on leaving the headquarters building he decided to look in at the Oriental Hotel, no more than five minutes walk away.

There was no reason whatever to question the arrangements made by his staff for the protection of the British Ambassador, and at the back of Otani's mind there was the notion that, by delaying his arrival, he could ensure that Rosie Winchmore would be well clear of the bathroom. He had no more scruples about holding up the evening meal than any other Japanese husband. Whether he turned up at seven or ten in the evening, he knew that Hanae would have his supper ready almost by the time he had settled down in the living-room.

The New Year holidays well and truly over at last, downtown Kobe had reverted to normal, and there was plenty of bustle in the main streets where the shops routinely stayed open till nine in the evening. As he passed the Daimaru Department Store he made a mental note to remind Hanae to take back some of their unwanted New Year gifts, as most people did, and exchange them for coupons to the same value to be spent on other goods in the store. He was particularly anxious to get rid of the ornately embroidered orange house slippers sent by De-

89

tective Junko Migishima and her husband, a rank and file patrolman serving as a plainclothes assistant to Kimura, not to mention the cufflinks presented by Kimura himself. When manufacturers took the trouble to put buttons on shirt-sleeves, Otani saw no need to gild the lily.

He had just paused in front of a display of Morozoff chocolates in a confectionery shop window with the vague idea of buying some for Hanae to share with Rosie when he felt a hand on his arm and, turning, saw the young lady in question grinning broadly at him.

"Otani-san! What a nice surprise!" Otani bowed a little awkwardly, for Rosie was not alone. She was indeed quite openly holding hands with a young man, a foreigner like herself. Both were wearing jeans and what Otani thought of as running shoes but which in recent years seemed to have become normal footwear for anyone under the age of twenty-five. Over a T-shirt with the large Chinese character for "Good Fortune" emblazoned on it in red, Rosie wore a large shaggy knitted waistcoat which drooped almost to her knees, while her escort had on a bright blue plastic padded jacket over a roll-necked sweater.

Rosie was not very skilled in the social graces and became stuck in repetitive expressions of surprise at seeing her host; until the young man at her side let go of her hand, bowed and intervened in pleasantly courteous Japanese.

"How do you do, sir. I am honoured to meet you. Thank you for your many kindnesses to Winchmore-san." He pronounced the name correctly, as *Uinchimoa*. "My name is Casey."

Otani had no idea how common a name *Keishii* might be, but was distinctly jolted by hearing it for the second time that day. "How do you do. I am pleased to meet you. You speak Japanese very well. May I ask if you are a fellow student of Rosie-san at London University?"

At this Rosie found her tongue again. "Oh, no. That is,

he *was*. But Patrick was in his final year when I started. And now he's a tea ceremony master, what do you think about that?''

Otani muttered clichés as he surveyed the young man with very keen interest. Patrick Casey was, for a foreigner, a pleasant-enough-looking sort of person. Under the bulky jacket he seemed to be slightly built, and was not much taller than Otani himself—perhaps 170 or 172 centimetres, Otani thought. He now knew that Casey was twenty-three years old, but thought that he looked older, since there was a thinness about his soft hair which augured baldness within comparatively few years. His demeanour was gentle, and his features, though thin, were well-modelled and regular. In normal circumstances Otani left such judgements to Kimura but, temporarily bereft of his support, he came to the rapid conclusion that Patrick Casey did not on the face of it look like the stuff of which assassins' accomplices are made.

On the other hand, what was he doing in Kobe? Otani wanted very much to know, but this casual encounter scarcely gave him the opportunity to find out. Rosie's remark at least called for some sort of response, so Otani professed admiring surprise and waited to see what would happen next. In fact Casey seemed embarrassed, and hastened to modify Rosie's enthusiasm.

''Hardly that,'' he said. ''At least, not yet.'' His Japanese was really very easy and assured. ''I've been studying the tea ceremony for some years now, and was privileged to be accepted as a pupil by Minamikuni-sensei, the head of the Southern School. The late head, I should say. Unfortunately he died very tragically the other day.''

''I know,'' Otani said briefly. At this point Rosie burst in again.

''He was *there*, Pat!'' she cried in English as Otani looked on uncomprehendingly. ''And never said a word

91

about it when they got home!'' She turned to Otani and reverted to her eccentric Japanese. ''You didn't tell me about it,'' she said reproachfully. ''I had to find out from the paper. And Patrick told me today.''

The three of them constituted a significant obstacle to the flow of passers-by on the narrow sidewalk, obstructed as it was anyway by displays spilling out from the shops on the one hand and the massive electricity supply poles, which disfigure every Japanese town and city, on the other. People strolling by made their way round them tolerantly enough, but Otani came to a bold and adventurous decision, and asked the two young people if they would like a cup of coffee. Rosie hesitated, but Patrick Casey not at all, and they were soon crowded round a tiny table in Coffee Etoile.

Otani asked his guests purely as a matter of form whether they would like anything to eat. Rosie declined with a shudder, gazing round her in horror at the other patrons busily demolishing huge toasted sandwiches, elaborate cakes and, in the case of one diminutive girl in a miniskirt, a mountain of American-style hotcakes drenched in syrup and surmounted by a ring of canned pineapple, the whole liberally anointed with whipped cream. Casey also turned down his offer, but Otani thought he detected some regret in his manner.

The service was, as always, prompt and efficient, and there was little necessity to revert to the conversation outside the coffee shop until Otani and Casey were stirring their cups of strong blended coffee and Rosie was sipping at her lemon tea. Then Otani spoke directly to Casey. ''You know of course that I am a police officer?''

He nodded. ''Yes. Winchmore-san, I mean Rosie-san wrote to me to say that she was coming to Japan and that you and your wife had kindly offered to have her to stay with you.''

Then Otani turned to Rosie. ''We didn't say anything

about what happened on Sunday when we arrived home, not wishing to trouble you. Of course my wife and I had no idea that your friend was at the tea ceremony." He sat back as Rosie and Patrick Casey spoke to each other in English, watching their faces.

"I understand that you were assisting," he went on when the private exchange seemed to be over. "Handing round the cakes. I must admit I didn't notice you."

Casey smiled. "Oh, I wasn't allowed to go into the actual room. I was outside the fusuma, just helping to carry cakes from the preparation room at the back."

Otani nodded with a sense of relief. He would indeed have been slipping badly had he failed to notice a *gaijin* among the attendants, even in traditional Japanese dress. "This sad event must have interrupted your studies," he said, and Casey nodded.

"I had been staying at the school as the guest of the Iemoto, but of course I moved out." Otani saw that he and Rosie were holding hands again, and felt quite put out on behalf of Roger, the bus-conductor back in London.

"Well, I mustn't intrude any longer," he said after finishing his coffee and picking up the bill, then added rather tentatively to Rosie, "Will you be back for supper this evening? It's getting rather late . . ."

Rosie shook her head and smiled. "No, I don't think so, thank you. Patrick and I have plans. Don't wait up . . . oh, thanks for the tea." Casey struggled to his feet and bowed as Otani stood up, conscious of having been dismissed, and not a little concerned over Rosie's moral welfare.

Back in the street he hesitated, then decided to continue on to the Oriental Hotel. Inside the lobby he looked round, half expecting to see a uniformed policeman on duty there. Instead he spotted the hefty figure of Patrolman Migishima, one of the few junior members of his headquarters staff whom he had good reason to know very well. Migishima was in what looked like agitated conversation with a man in a black jacket and striped trousers, evidently a member of the managerial staff.

Otani sauntered over. "Good evening," he said quietly, and Migishima turned, recognised him and immediately stood rigidly to attention. Although in civilian clothes he might just as well have been wearing a placard round his neck announcing his profession, and Otani sighed inwardly. "Everything in order, Migishima?" The young man's eyes rolled horribly while the hotel functionary looked on, a worried look on his face. It was fairly clear to Otani that something was amiss, so he began to move off, speaking as he did so to the man in the formal suit. "Excuse us for a moment. Step over here, would you, Migishima?" Migishima hurriedly followed him to an unfrequented corner of the lobby, near a display of airline timetables in a wire rack. "And do relax. We don't want to make ourselves conspicuous. Now, what's the trouble?"

Migishima looked as though he wished the ground would open up and swallow him.

"Pull yourself together, man!" Otani was becoming quite alarmed. "Has something happened to the ambassador?"

Migishima at last regained the power of speech. "No, sir. At least . . . that is, he's quite all right at the moment, sir."

"What do you mean, *at the moment*?" Migishima gulped, and removed from his inner pocket a plastic bag, which Otani could see contained one of the Oriental Hotel's own envelopes, with some typing on the front. He took out his glasses and peered at it.

"It's correctly addressed to the British Ambassador, sir," Migishima said. "Sir Rodney Hurtling, KCMG, British Ambassador, care of Oriental Hotel, Kobe. Er, if you would look at the other side, sir." Otani turned the plastic bag over, and saw that a slip of paper had been placed so

94

that what was written on it could be read without the necessity to touch it.

It was the usual method—words and letters cut out of a newspaper, in this case an English language edition. "What does it say, Migishima?"

"It's a threat, sir. I'm very sorry, sir." Catching the warning glint in Otani's eye, the young man cleared his throat. "It says in effect, 'You were lucky. Next time we'll make certain.' There's no signature, sir."

"And this actually reached the ambassador?"

"I'm afraid so, sir. It was slipped under his door, it seems. Some time about an hour ago, His Excellency thinks. The ambassador called the manager, and when you arrived I was just trying to find out how it was delivered."

"Don't we have a man on duty in the corridor outside his door?"

Migishima hung his head. "No, sir. I'm sorry, sir. There are three European ambassadors staying here, and we simply don't have the manpower to provide twenty-four-hour protection for them. We have someone here in the lobby at all times, and the hotel security staff have orders to patrol the corridors concerned at least every half-hour."

"I see. I'll speak to the manager myself." Otani was profoundly concerned, but told himself that the security measures in force were not on the whole unreasonable. Only in the case of senior members of the Imperial Family and visiting Heads of State or Government was saturation coverage possible. That was because the Emperor himself and those closest to him travelled with a phalanx of Imperial Household Agency chamberlains and their own police guards, while guests of the Japanese Government were also provided with personal protection everywhere they went in Japan.

What worried Otani most was not that he would be obliged to order a maximum alert for the following day's ceremony, but the fact that Patrick Casey had been in the vicinity of the Oriental Hotel at what was stated to have been the material time.

And Rosie Winchmore had been with him.

Chapter 12

OTANI TURNED OVER RESTLESSLY AND PEERED IN THE darkness at the luminous hands of the small clock poised within reach at his side of the bedding which Hanae placed directly on the tatami matting every night and stowed away in the big built-in cupboard in the mornings. Two twenty-five. It was hopeless. Sleep was out of the question, with Rosie not having yet come back to the house. After lying on his back for a while, Otani rolled quietly out, shuddering as the chill of the room struck his nudity, and hurriedly finding and putting on the lined yukata he had flung down on going to bed at a little before eleven. Then he paused and listened to Hanae's even breathing before creeping stealthily out of the room and down the stairs.

Left to herself, Hanae tried to decide what to do. She was, needless to say, wide-awake herself, but better able to disguise the fact than her husband. She was also worried to death about Rosie, but not for the same reasons as Otani. From the moment she had been told by their daughter Akiko during their visit to London that Rosie's parents were

97

divorced and that Rosie lived, with or without their approval, openly with a lover called Roger, she had found it difficult to come to terms with such flagrant flouting of conventions. That Rosie was now out in the middle of the night somewhere in Kobe in the company of a completely different young man, according to her husband, was positively alarming.

After two or three minutes of indecision, Hanae too got out of bed and went downstairs, first turning on the electric fan heater to take the chill off the upstairs room. The previous summer the Otanis had thought seriously about getting an air conditioner, but, being like most Japanese more concerned with keeping cool than with keeping warm, had never even considered the possibility of central heating. Hanae found her husband hovering in the kitchen, the refrigerator door open.

"Are you hungry?" she enquired quietly, and Otani jumped.

"I didn't hear you come down," he said accusingly. "No, not particularly. I couldn't sleep, though."

"Nor can I. Would you like some tea?" Otani nodded and Hanae quickly made some green tea and took it with a packet of rice and seaweed crackers into the living-room. After crunching his way through one of the brittle crackers and sipping at his tea appreciatively, Otani sighed.

"Nearly a quarter to three."

Hanae sighed in turn. "Yes. What *could* she be doing?"

Otani raised an eyebrow. "What do you think? I can only suggest one thing. She must be in a love hotel with that young man."

Hanae frowned. She was not alarmed over Rosie's physical safety in law-abiding Japan, where a woman may walk alone in any of the big cities at night without fear, and where violence is almost exclusively either domestic or

98

confined to those involved in or on the fringes of organised crime. Hanae had only once visited one of the so-called "love" hotels which let rooms—often furnished and equipped in an exotic or bizarre way—by the hour to couples, and then in the company of her own husband; but she had learned through that experience how numerous and well-patronised they were. She had indeed read quite recently in one of the weekly magazines in the beauty shop that new hotels of this type were springing up everywhere, representing with Turkish baths and massage parlours one of the principal boom sectors in the otherwise sluggish Japanese economy.

"You said he seemed quite pleasant," Hanae said rather despairingly. "And surely, Rosie-san has that nice young man in London . . ." Her voice trailed off and she shook her head worriedly, not really persuading herself. Hanae had few illusions about sex, and was in a sense unshockable. She was, however, a conventional middle-aged lady in most ways, and had been imbued from childhood with the conviction that nice girls don't; or at least that they shouldn't let it be known if they do. Rosie's apparent unconcern about maintaining before her hosts the appearance of respectability bothered Hanae much more than the idea that she was probably in bed with a comparatively casual friend at that moment.

She was troubled, too, by her husband's behaviour. He had come home unusually late the previous evening in a heavy, uncommunicative mood, quite obviously worried about something, but rebuffing her tentative attempts to get him to talk to her. He had reported tersely that he had met Rosie in the company of a young foreigner in Kobe, that they had dropped into a coffee shop for a while, and that Rosie had indicated that she might be late back. It sounded like an interesting encounter to Hanae and she would have been glad to hear more, but Otani had been unco-operative. After picking at his evening meal he had hunched gloomily

99

in front of the television except for making two telephone calls and receiving one, then taken himself off to bed with scarcely another word. Yet he had not seemed upset with her; just totally preoccupied.

Nights were very quiet usually, since the street in which their old house stood was the last before the built-up area gave up the struggle against the shaggy, precipitous slopes of Mount Rokko, so the sound of the taxi was audible to them long before it reached the house and drew up outside. Hanae gazed at her husband in mingled relief and confusion, then quickly got up and made for the stairs. "*You* talk to her," she instructed Otani as the passenger door banging shut was heard, and had scuttled away before the taxi even moved off.

For a moment Otani was strongly tempted to follow his wife's timid example, but then remembered that the front door was locked and that Rosie would be unable to get in without his assistance. He pulled himself together, tidied his yukata, and unscrewed the bolt on the sliding outer door just before it was rattled open and Rosie stepped in. She looked up at her host, standing as he was on the upper level like a figure of doom, and smiled nervously.

"Oh," she said. "I thought you'd be in bed."

"I *was* in bed," Otani said pointedly. "You are very late, Rosie-san."

"Yes, I know. May I come in, please?" Otani stood to one side as Rosie took off her shoes and stepped up into the house, then re-locked the door and followed her into the living-room.

"My wife was very worried about you," he said. "She would like you to be back by, say, ten or ten-thirty while you are staying with us." He was really just playing for time while wondering what line to take with the English girl, and was astonished by her reaction to what sounded to him like an entirely reasonable and straightforward stip-

100

ulation. A look of incredulity spread over her face, and she gaped at him in stupefaction.

"You must be joking! I . . . *ten-thirty*?"

"My wife feels responsible for you," he added lamely, keeping his voice low in the hope that Hanae would not overhear him so shamelessly attributing all the fuss to her, and not for the first time in his career was completely at a loss. After the bombshell of the threatening letter to the British Ambassador and the anxious expostulations of the manager of the hotel to the effect that he had arranged for a member of his own staff to keep continuous watch in the corridor outside the room for the remainder of the night, Otani had made no attempt to contact the ambassador himself, preferring to leave that inevitably disagreeable task to Kimura or to Ambassador Atsugi, both of whom he had alerted by telephone.

Migishima insisted, and Otani could see from the brevity of the message, that the threat was unspecific. There was therefore no particular reason to assume that the next attempt on Sir Rodney Hurtling's life would take place at the opening of the trade fair, beyond the fact that he would once more be in a specific place at a prescribed time. Manpower shortage or no manpower shortage, Otani had ordered that additional men from his own force should be assigned to the Oriental Hotel to supplement the hotel's efforts to boost security there overnight, and that from the moment the ambassador and his wife left the premises until their departure from Osaka Airport the next day they were to be fully protected by armed bodyguards.

It had been impossible to do anything that evening about Casey, even if Otani had wanted to try. He had no idea where he and Rosie might be likely to have gone after he left them, and in any case had nothing objective to support the obvious suspicion that must fall upon Casey. The actual letter and envelope might conceivably yield fingerprints, but he doubted if they would. It was not difficult to come by one of the hotel's envelopes, nor to get access to a typewriter. Otani certainly intended to put some questions to Casey in due course, and would not hesitate to have him arrested if he were found anywhere in the ambassador's proximity the next day, but that did not help him in his present predicament, with Rosie glaring at him in his own living-room, her face flushed. He felt he had to go on as he had begun.

"You see, before our daughter was married she used to come home by ten." Otani forbore to add that when Akiko had been involved in radical student politics—and almost certainly having an affair with the man she later married—she had frequently not come home at all. When Akiko *did* sleep at home, though, she had been scrupulous to be there by locking-up time.

"I'm not your daughter," Rosie pointed out tersely. "And I'm not used to being treated like a child. I won't trouble you again. I'll leave first thing in the morning." Now her lip was quivering, and she looked more tearful than angry. Otani knew quite well that he was mishandling her hopelessly. Quite apart from anything else, if the girl had been enthusiastically making love for a couple of hours as he had suggested to Hanae and indeed thought quite likely, she probably needed some sleep. She certainly looked more than a little bedraggled, and when she took off the woolly waistcoat Otani noticed a red mark on her neck which looked to him as though it had been made by human teeth. It reassured him just a little. Better to think that the young Irish tea master had been inflicting love-bites than that he had been involved in the past few hours in setting up a political assassination.

"Please don't do that," Otani said insincerely. In fact he wished more than ever he had not been so foolish as to invite the wretched girl to stay with them, and considered that it would be an excellent idea for her to go away. He knew that Hanae would never forgive him if she did, though, and realised that they would both lose face most horribly if Rosie were to leave prematurely and in an atmosphere of ill-will. Moreover, he dreaded to think what Akiko and her husband in London would have to say about it all when it got back to them. "It's very late, and I am sure there has been a misunderstanding. Er, has Casey-san gone back to Kyoto?"

Rosie did not look in the least mollified. "What do you want to know for?" she demanded. Otani was not used to being challenged so peremptorily by anyone, let alone a young woman, and had to swallow his irritation.

"I simply thought . . . well, there are no trains after midnight," he said, not achieving the matter-of-fact tone he was aiming at.

"Look, I'm going to bed, OK?" Rosie had lapsed into English, but Otani comprehended the significance of the word "bed" and the interrogative "OK?" and nodded silently, resigned to the fact that Casey's present whereabouts were going to remain unknown to him.

"I am very sorry, Rosie-san," Otani said as she went out of the room, presumably on the way to the bathroom. "Forgive me. We were both anxious about you."

Rosie turned and looked at him, still sullen and seemingly not far from tears. "It doesn't matter," she said, and disappeared.

The old house was in no way soundproof, and when Otani slipped back into bed he breathed rather than whispered into Hanae's ear. "Did you hear all that?"

"I heard," she breathed back, then turned ostentatiously away from him and firmly removed the hand he was trying to insinuate into the front of her yukata. Otani lay there unhappily, confirmed in his conviction that he had made a great mess of things, and wondering if, by some remote and almost unbelievable chance, Rosie had been in Kyoto on the fatal Sunday afternoon.

Chapter 13

"YOU SEE, CHIEF, THEY REALLY DO COME IN ALL shapes and sizes, just like us,'' Kimura pointed out in an undertone as he and Otani stood on the edge of the small crowd of a hundred or so invited guests at the opening ceremony of the European Commission Trade Fair, otherwise known as EUREXPORT—TOWARDS THE TWENTY-FIRST CENTURY, as Kimura obligingly translated for Otani from the large streamer draped on the wall beneath a colourful multitude of national flags at the Trade Centre near Kobe Harbour.

Otani nodded abstractedly. He felt depressed, headachy and on edge after his wretched night and watched without much interest. It was true enough that the ten foreigners who stood in an ill-disciplined line behind a long red and white ribbon, each holding a pair of scissors handed to him previously on a lacquer tray by his own personal Miss Kobe in her smart cherry-red suit, high-heeled shoes and white gloves, constituted a pretty mixed bag. Sir Rodney Hurtling was the tallest, but there was a cadaverous bean-pole of a man at one end of the line who towered almost as

105

high, and looked particularly odd in relation to his neighbour, who was tubby and short, and sweating profusely. All ten wore glasses, and all had affixed to their jackets large imitation chrysanthemum rosettes from which trailed ribbons with their designations written on them in Chinese characters with a felt-tip pen. Thin, fat, tall, short, bald, moustachioed and in one case even bearded, they gave the lie to Otani's firm conviction that all Westerners look alike, particularly about the eyes.

"There aren't as many guests here as I'd imagined there would be," Otani said as the Governor of Hyogo Prefecture, having completed his speech of welcome, nodded benignly at the envoys, poised as they were for the snip, and flashbulbs began to pop. It was not well done. About half of the team managed to cut through the ribbon more or less at the same time, but one fat man contrived to wedge the material in his scissors and thus pull it out of those of his neighbours on either side. Sir Rodney Hurtling dropped his altogether and, slightly flushed, cut his ribbon length a good half minute later, after his Miss Kobe had retrieved them for him, and by which time the ripple of applause had largely subsided and the majority of the guests were making for the abundant refreshments laid out on long tables at one side of the exhibition area.

"A lot will come for the food and drink now that the speeches are finished," Kimura predicted confidently. "Even so, I think the riskiest time is over now. All invitation cards are being thoroughly checked at the reception desk, and Press photographers with bulky equipment have all been searched. Quite apart from that, we've got over a dozen plain-clothesmen in here as well as a few men on the roof and around the building. Nothing really that can be done about a gunman who doesn't care if he's caught, but judging by the Kyoto performance that's not our man's style."

Otani nodded again, reflecting that at least Kimura was

right about the late arrivals. The crowd was already half as large again as it had been during the speeches, and it was becoming difficult to get at any of the food for the crush at the tables. He looked in the direction of the British Ambassador and was reassured to see that two tough-looking men in dark suits were keeping close to him and looking around warily as he talked animatedly to the Governor.

"You know, I really get the impression that he's almost enjoying having to have all this protection," Kimura said at Otani's elbow. "He seemed in a perfectly good mood when I spoke to him earlier."

Otani had hardly realised that Kimura had been away, and was pleasantly surprised to see that he was now being offered a plate of *sushi* by him. In spite of his feeling of malaise, his mouth watered as he took it and looked at the five mouthfuls of seasoned rice, including one topped with shrimp, one with octopus tentacle and one with eel. "You even remembered the ginger pickle," Otani said gratefully as he accepted the pair of chopsticks Kimura now took in their paper wrapper from his breast pocket and handed over.

"I've got a German sausage and sauerkraut," Kimura replied, showing his superior the peculiar-looking contents of his own plate. "I'm afraid you'll have to get your own drink if you want one, though."

Otani could see several people he knew, including three members of his own Rotary Club, but doubted if anyone of his acquaintance would approach him, since he was in uniform. Although not entirely happy about eating in the circumstances, he thought he was fairly safe for a few minutes and in any case was quite unable to resist the sushi.

Once he had disposed of it, he straightened his tunic and resumed his most official face. "What will they do now, Kimura?" he asked, savouring the aftertaste of the pungent green horseradish paste used to bring out the flavour of the fish. "Go round the exhibits?"

"You really ought to try some of the other food," Kimura said. "I'm quite surprised that they actually had sushi. It's mainly European, you see, for obvious reasons. Ravioli from Italy, snails from France, smoked salmon from Britain, the German sausages, and so on."

Otani drew himself up. "Inspector Kimura, may I remind you that we are here on duty? If you're still hungry when we leave, I will personally buy you some lunch. It's not even eleven yet."

Kimura was not really crushed, but looked slightly embarrassed as he hastily put his plate down on a nearby table and cleared his throat. "Ah. Yes, of course. Well. The British Ambassador is supposed to leave here at eleven-fifteen. I imagine he'll take a quick turn round the exhibition soon, but of course all the VIPs saw it in the half-hour before the opening. Then straight to Osaka Airport and back to Tokyo by plane, as you know. His own car is already on the way back to Tokyo on the highway. The Governor has made transport available all the way to the airport and of course our people will be escorting the cars. The Frenchman and the Italian are going back on the same plane. Incidentally, the Italian Ambassador's wife is a real stunner. That's her—the blonde over there."

"The Osaka police have of course been alerted?" There was iron in Otani's quiet voice, and Kimura cleared his throat again.

"Yes, sir," he replied soberly. "Naturally. I was in touch with Ambassador Atsugi's office earlier, and he'll be seeing the ambassadors off. Osaka police have maximum security coverage at Itami airport, even though I somehow doubt if any attempt will be made on Sir Rodney there. After all, the travelling arrangements weren't publicised, whereas this opening ceremony here is getting the full Press treatment."

Otani looked around him. There were still far more people clustered round the tables laden with exotic titbits than looking round the exhibits, but already numbers of guests

108

were making their way towards the exits having eaten their fill. Three photographers remained of the troop who had been there to cover the actual ribbon-cutting ceremony, and these were dogging the movements of the more senior ambassadors and of the undoubtedly beauteous Italian lady, snapping them in conversation with local commercial and political notables.

All at once Otani felt that he was wasting his time amid this colourful tomfoolery, and wanted to be off. He turned to Kimura. "I'll leave you to finish up the food," he said, noticing his hungry gaze fixed on the tables, by no means yet denuded of their burden. "I'm going back to the office. Let me know when the ambassador is safely out of Hyogo Prefecture. Then I think I'll go to Kyoto again."

Kimura was surprised, and it showed on his face. "Oh?"

"Yes. I've got a murder to investigate. Perhaps you'd forgotten." Otani immediately regretted his tart manner and smiled at Kimura. "Sorry. I shouldn't snap at you. You've done a good job here, Kimura-kun. But it's struck me that I should have paid more attention to what Ambassador Atsugi pointed out. The British Ambassador spends most of his time in Tokyo, you see."

Kimura fingered the exquisite knot of his silk tie from the Turnbull and Asser boutique in the Seibu Department Store in Tokyo. "Well, obviously he does," he said in some bewilderment.

Otani stared at him. "Well, then. Why go to all the trouble to arrange an exceedingly complicated assassination—a *blind* assassination, in a sense—in Kyoto, or here in Kobe for that matter, when it would be a lot easier to mark his movements in Tokyo?"

Kimura shrugged his expensively-tailored shoulders. Now that Otani had announced his intention of leaving, he wished he would go. Quite apart from the food which remained, Kimura was anxious to make the acquaintance of one or two foreign girls in various styles of national dress who were in attendance, and if possible pay his respects to the Italian Ambassadress. "I really couldn't say. Presumably the Metropolitan Police have pretty effective protection arrangements up there. Easier to get him in Kyoto, especially with this fellow Casey in place to help with the proceedings."

Otani sighed. "You may be right. Anyway, I leave it to you to take charge here and see the Ambassador safely away."

As he turned aside, the receiver in his tunic pocket emitted a bleeping sound, and Otani hastily made for a corner of the big exhibition hall, positioning himself unobtrusively behind a pillar as he fixed the small speaker into his ear and took out the instrument to acknowledge the call signal. It was of the newest type, no bigger than a packet of cigarettes, and the fine cord to the earpiece served as its aerial. There were other uniformed officers here and there in the hall in addition to the plain-clothesmen, and these were openly equipped with the larger, conventional walkie-talkies and earpieces.

The message from prefectural police headquarters for Otani was very simple, and consisted of two parts. First, he was informed that Patrick Casey had not slept at his modest hotel in Kyoto the previous night, and that his key was still in its pigeonhole at the reception desk. Second, that he was requested to call a certain number urgently.

The number, he knew, would be that of a public telephone from which Woman Detective Junko Migishima wished to report to him personally, as he had instructed her to do early that morning. The departure of Inspector Sakamoto had made it not only very easy but indeed perfectly logical for Otani to assume personal charge of the Criminal Investigation Section and to assign the members of its staff to such duties as he thought fit, without the necessity to confide in either Noguchi or Kimura.

That they would find out sooner or later was of no importance. What was important was that Otani should have Rosie Winchmore tailed from the time she left their house at Rokko. If she met Patrick Casey, he would have to take certain disagreeable steps. If she didn't, it would be a great relief.

Otani hastened to the nearest red public telephone in the entrance lobby, fumbling for some ten-yen coins as he did so.

Chapter 14

OTANI HAD NEVER BEEN MUCH OF A ONE FOR NIGHT life, and since achieving lonely eminence as officer commanding the Hyogo Prefectural Police Force could probably have counted on the fingers of his two hands the number of times he had been out in the evening in sociable company with colleagues. Even those occasions were usually in Tokyo where he went several times a year for conferences or briefings at the National Police Agency and was sometimes prevailed upon to make the rounds of a few bars with some of his old acquaintances working in the Agency or in the Metropolitan force.

Even now, he told himself, he was really on duty, but nevertheless looked around him with lively interest as Noguchi proceeded in a stately way down the street known as Kiyamachi in the central entertainment area of Kyoto, a stone's throw from the Pontocho geisha quarter. In spite of the pleasantly unpolluted stream fringed with willow trees which ran alongside the street, the establishments which lined the other side were a far cry from the discreet and exclusive geisha houses in Pontocho itself or in the equally well-known Gion area fifteen minutes walk to the southwest.

It was just before nine in the evening, and the touts in their sharp dinner suits were in full cry outside almost every building, most of which housed anything from two or three to a dozen or more bars or so-called cabarets and pink salons. Otani was perfectly well aware of what went on in the last-named, staffed by amateur "hostesses" who might be anything from bored or hard-up married women to high-school girls. Every large city had plenty of pink salons, which occupied a position very near the end of the market and which provided at modest cost gaudy facilities and complaisant women for boozy groping, quite unlike the stylish but expensive elegance of the best type of bar. Nevertheless, it was the first time Otani could recall having been in Kyoto by night, and even the cheap and tawdry side of Kiyamachi had a certain air to it which marked it off as different from Kobe.

"Off your hands, then, is he?" Noguchi had been silent for quite a long time, and it took Otani a moment to decide whether his old friend was referring to the British Ambassador or perhaps to Inspector Sakamoto. He inferred that it must be the former.

"Yes. Kimura reported that the departure from Osaka Airport was completely uneventful. Just before I left to come here I had a call from Atsugi at the Foreign Ministry Liaison Office in Osaka to say that the Ambassador was safely back in Tokyo. It seems he has no plans to come this way again for some months, so at least we can concentrate on one thing at a time from now on."

Otani had changed into civilian clothes but still made a sharp contrast to the disreputable Noguchi, and the touts outside the buildings tended to fall temporarily silent and look at them warily as they passed.

"Had anything to eat?"

"Don't worry," Otani reassured him hastily, knowing

113

the sort of place Noguchi usually patronised. "Where are we meeting this contact of yours?" They had arrived at the Shijo boulevard, still alive with traffic and pedestrians even though the shutters were beginning to go up outside the big shops as they closed.

"Not far now." They waited for the traffic lights to change and crossed the busy street, still heading south, and continued down Kiyamachi, which became almost immediately darker, quieter and somehow more secretive than at its brassy northern end. There were fewer people about, and although there were for the first couple of hundred metres still a few restaurants and bars, the eating-houses were drab and cheap, and the bars were just that: simple counters at which customers stood, presided over by a middle-aged or elderly man or woman and devoted solely to the business of drinking.

A little way further down, Noguchi turned into a side alley barely wide enough to admit his bulk, and then at once into the entrance to an inn. It was a small, unpretentious inn in spite of its resounding name, which was the Pavilion of the Bamboo Dream, and obviously catered for low-budget travellers. Like the vast majority of Japanese, Otani was oblivious to the poetry of place names, surnames and names of business establishments, and found the Pavilion of the Bamboo Dream as a name no more noteworthy than a Londoner finds names like Cheapside, Earl's Court or Chalk Farm.

He was, however, relieved to see that the inn looked perfectly clean and decent, for all its modesty, and would not particularly have minded staying there. That would not be necessary, though, since before leaving Kobe he had telephoned to book himself into the Station Hotel, overcoming his prejudice against Western-style accommodation for the sake of the anonymity and freedom to come and go which could not be found in a Japanese inn. Hanae had been surprised and not best pleased to learn that he was intending to stay overnight in Kyoto anyway, and supposed that a desire to avoid another encounter with Rosie might have been a factor. Otani had not bothered to disabuse her.

Otani and Noguchi were met in the entrance to the inn by the proprietor, a bright-eyed woman whom Otani judged to be in her middle fifties. She was among the increasing minority of elderly Japanese of both sexes who scorn the use of dye to keep the hair black, and had a fine head of grey hair drawn back into a simple knot. Her kimono was of good quality and seemed to be in a subtle shade of grey-blue, but that might have been a trick of the dim light of the entrance.

Somewhat to Otani's surprise, Noguchi did not appear to know her, and introduced both himself and Otani by name but not rank or profession, addressing her politely as *oyanushi-san*.

"I was expecting you about now," she replied in a friendly way, displaying no trace of being intimidated by Noguchi's tough appearance. "My name is Uemura, at your service. This way, please."

The two men took off their shoes and followed her up a flight of polished wooden stairs to an upstairs room. It was of eight mats, a fair size, and was furnished with a low table of imitation lacquer and a pile of zabuton cushions in one corner. Mrs Uemura placed three of them round the table and gestured Otani to the place of honour in front of the rudimentary tokonoma alcove which had in it an arrangement of twigs in a flat dish that Otani guessed was in accordance with the style of the Sogetsu school of "flower arrangement" which in fact generally dispensed with the use of actual flowers. Its tastefulness struck him, but not so much as the fact that Mrs Uemura herself took the third cushion, kneeling formally on it with easy grace.

Noguchi had not specified the sex of his "contact" but on arrival at the inn Otani had quite expected to find someone other than the proprietor waiting to talk to them. "We won't be disturbed," she said. "Business is very quiet at this time of the year. There are only two guests staying here tonight and they've both gone to bed already, downstairs." Otani rather doubted it, since he could hear the sound of a television set coming from somewhere below, but in principle nine-fifteen was not an unreasonable time for people staying at a Japanese inn to have had their bath and evening meal and be settling down for the night.

In contradiction of Mrs Uemura's words, they were immediately disturbed, but only by a young maid with rosy cheeks, quite obviously fresh from the country, who brought a tray on which were a large vacuum flask of hot water, a canister of tea, a pot, three cups and three tiny plates, on each of which was a bean-jam cake wrapped in tissue paper. Mrs Uemura deftly made and served the tea as the girl withdrew and slid the fusuma door closed behind her, then fixed her attention on Noguchi.

"So," she said. "It has been a long time since police officers have entered this inn. My nephew says he owes you a favour, so you are welcome all the same." Noguchi, still seemingly on his best behaviour, gruffly disclaimed having been of any particular service to her nephew, and apologised for troubling her so late in the evening. Otani was at a loss how to proceed in what at best seemed likely to be a very tricky conversation, and was momentarily irritated with Noguchi for not having briefed him properly in advance, as well as with himself for not having asked any questions. He was given a lead by Mrs Uemura herself.

"So Fujiwara's in some kind of trouble," she said thoughtfully. "I'd never have supposed something that happened so long ago would come back to haunt him. Until I heard about the Iemoto being killed, that is." It took all of Otani's self-control to sip quietly at his tea, betraying nothing of the excitement he felt: Noguchi for his part had obviously withdrawn into a purely listening role and was unlikely to speak, though Otani knew that he would if necessary be able to repeat verbatim everything the woman said.

"How did you hear about it? Television? The papers?" Otani's question was put in a casual, matter-of-fact way, but seemed to amuse Mrs Uemura.

"What do *you* think? Why, I was one of the first to know. My baby tells me everything, and he was on the phone within an hour or so."

"Your baby?"

"I know I shouldn't call him that. I was only his wet-nurse after all. But I'm the only proper mother the young master ever had." There could in the circumstances be only one "young master". It was enough to enable Otani to risk moving forward and build on what promised to be a sure foundation.

"How long did you stay with the family after the baby was born?" Mrs Uemura closed her eyes in thought and Otani watched her, impressed by the refinement of her features. Then she opened them again, and Otani thought he saw pain.

"Just over five years," she said. "So it had been getting on for ten years in all. But I kept in touch on the quiet, and when he got a bit older my baby kept in touch with me. He made sure of that."

Otani did some rapid mental arithmetic. "The new Iemoto is thirty-two, I believe. So you first worked for the family over thirty-five years ago?"

"That's right. I was fifteen when they sent me from the country . . . oh, a clumsy child I was, too." A reminiscent smile flitted over her face. "Working as a maid in the Minamikuni house soon taught me a thing or two, though. After a year or so I think I could have passed as a daughter except for my clothes. Of course, I *am* a distant cousin, after all."

Otani said nothing, willing her to go on, and delighted

117

with the information that was tumbling out. With his love for hypothesising he had already thought of at least three possible ways in which Fujiwara might come into the picture in due course, all of them wrong.

"And I stayed until Her Ladyship insisted that I had to go. Said people were talking. I ask you! As though there'd ever been a time when people weren't talking! You know what Kyoto's like."

Thus appealed to, Otani nodded. He certainly knew of the reputation of Kyoto gossip, much of it elegantly malicious. "So you married?"

"Yes. They found me a husband and set us up in this place. He wasn't much use and I got rid of him a couple of years later."

"Still, it was quite generous of them, I suppose." Otani looked around the room. A simple inn in an unfashionable part of Kyoto might not represent a gold-mine, but was hardly to be sniffed at. He was therefore surprised when Mrs Uemura did in fact sniff and he noticed that the smile on her face was of a different kind from that he had seen earlier. It confirmed the impression he had formed that the proprietor of the Pavilion of the Bamboo Dream was a tough lady.

"Thank you," he said. "That's very helpful to know. So you were in a position to find out a lot about the whole family, and their friends." He was hoping very hard that she would bring the name of Fujiwara back into the conversation, and cursing himself for not having arranged to have a little elementary research done on the recent history of the Minamikuni family. He had no idea when the late Grand Master had succeeded to the headship of the Southern School; nor did he know anything about the background of the lady who was now his widow.

"Indeed I was," Mrs Uemura said, the strange smile still in place, and lapsed into silence. Otani was not too worried by this, since during his long and successful career

118

as an interrogator he had found on many occasions that most people are uneasy when the questioner himself falls silent and soon volunteer something, often startlingly indiscreet. Mrs Uemura was so obviously relishing some memory or other that it seemed sooner or later she would want to share it.

"I certainly was. Of course, the sensei had become Iemoto very young—barely old enough to handle the job, even with a lot of help. I don't know what they'd have done if the old man had died a year or two earlier. But he soon showed what he was made of." Otani sat back, content to let the woman make the running: Noguchi for his part might have been carved from stone, sitting there massively motionless, his tea and cake untouched.

"Even so, he couldn't marry as he really wanted to. Oh, no. The family would never have put up with that. It had to be arranged, needless to say. I felt sorry for her at first. She was no happier than he was about it. She was really in love with Fujiwara, you see."

Otani was jolted into speech. "Really! I see."

The woman looked at him sharply. "No, you don't. They were just a pair of children. The sensei was twenty-six and . . . well, I'd been making him happy for the past four years or so. There were times when I dreamed . . . and I think he did too . . ." Mrs Uemura made a gesture of irritation. "Then they found this young girl for him. Seventeen she was, younger than me. Just finishing high school, but good family, oh, my word, very good. And head over heels in love with young Fujiwara. It would have been just as good a match, except that the Fujiwaras didn't have the money to go with the name, and the Minamikunis did."

"So the marriage took place." Otani kept his voice flat and neutral.

"Yes, it took place." The pain was back in Mrs Uemura's eyes, and she paused for a while. "It took place just

119

after I found I was pregnant—'' She stopped abruptly, opened her eyes wide and placed a hand in front of her mouth. ''That's enough about that,'' she said then. It was clear that she regretted what she had said, and Otani tried to help her over the painful silence.

''Let me reassure you that your personal affairs are entirely confidential and will be treated as such. It's Fujiwara I'm interested in. Did he try to maintain contact with Mrs Minamikuni after her marriage?''

The owner of the Pavilion of the Bamboo Dream sighed heavily. ''He tried, yes. And I tried to help him, and I make no apology for that. But it was too difficult. And of course after a few months it was out of the question, anyway, when it became obvious. The baby, I mean.''

''I see. She became pregnant soon after the marriage?'' Otani experienced a flash of sympathy for the young, newlywed Grand Master, sharing a household with *two* young women he had made pregnant, his wife, and his maid and long-time mistress. The smile was resigned this time, and Mrs Uemura shook her head slowly. ''No. She became pregnant before the marriage. By Fujiwara.''

Chapter 15

"**A**LL RIGHT, SO SHE'S GONE," OTANI SNAPPED AND Hanae looked at him in open anger.

"And that's all you have to say about it? *You* invited her here, *you* made it quite obvious that she wasn't welcome, and *you* drove her out by your clumsiness!"

In over thirty years of marriage Otani and Hanae had their coolnesses and occasional flare-ups, but they were rare and invariably made Otani's stomach hurt. He paused in the act of removing his shoes and looked up at his wife, looming over him in the little entrance hall. Her anger and distress struck to his heart. He straightened up, one foot still shod, the other tentatively feeling for the wooden step up. "I'm sorry," he said simply. "I'm truly sorry."

The ritual of arriving home after any absence, whether following a normal day's work or even a couple of hours' stroll, was a minor joy of his life. His cry of "I'm back!" as he rattled open the sliding outer door and the immediate response of "Welcome home!" from Hanae wherever she was in the house, the words were automatic but none the

121

less precious for that, and her silence on this occasion had been like a whiplash.

Hanae withdrew to the living-room, leaving Otani to take off his other shoe and follow her sheepishly. "I'll go and see her in Nagoya and apologise. I'll explain that it was all a misunderstanding," he said to Hanae's back. He hoped very much that it was. The fact that Woman Detective Junko Migishima had tailed Rosie and her luggage to Kobe Station and watched her buy a ticket to Nagoya was reassuring, but the fact that Rosie had been met before passing through the barrier by a young man answering Casey's description and spent fifteen minutes in what was described to Otani as a seemingly tense and furtive conversation over a cup of tea with him in the snack bar was less so. It was a pity that by the time he had spoken to Junko Migishima and instructed her to tail Casey instead, the young man had disappeared.

"Hanae! I need to talk to you," he said when she continued to ignore him. "I need your advice. It has a bearing on the killing of the Iemoto in Kyoto. And it's a lot more important than whether or not I have offended an inconsiderate young woman like Rosie-san." His remorse was rapidly giving place to renewed irritation, and he was on the point of launching into a self-justification of his words and actions when Hanae reluctantly turned to face him. Her expression was still cold, but she no longer seemed quite so angry.

Otani started talking, describing his visit to Kyoto and his meeting with the late Grand Master's former mistress. He made no attempt to dramatise the story Mrs Uemura had told him, but related it baldly and economically, leaving out any mention of Fujiwara's name. Even so, Hanae's eyes widened as he went on and about halfway through his narrative she sank down onto a cushion, unconsciously indicating another so that he was encouraged to follow suit, still talking.

122

"So what I need to know is this," he concluded. "Could a maid in a house like that know for sure that the young bride was already pregnant when she was married—unless her new mistress had confided in her, I mean? Or could it be pure fantasy on the part of a jealous girl, herself pregnant by the young woman's husband?"

Hanae rubbed her forehead gently before answering. "Let me make sure I understand the situation. Are you telling me that this woman in the inn is really the mother of the new Grand Master?"

Otani shook his head. "No. Either she lost her baby at birth, or she has a son or daughter of almost exactly his age. She *nursed* the new Iemoto. What we don't know is who his father was. Plenty of brides conceive on their wedding night. If this girl had been made pregnant just a week or two beforehand, it wouldn't necessarily give rise to comment when the baby was born—a couple of weeks' prematurity isn't anything remarkable."

Hanae pondered. "The bride was just seventeen, you said?"

"Yes."

"Well, with people of that background it would be absolutely understood that the girl would be expected to be a virgin. A personal maid ought to be able to tell after the wedding night whether or not that was the case, unless the couple went away for a honeymoon. Needless to say, the husband ought to be able to tell, too; but men can be surprisingly ignorant."

Otani nodded, wrily remembering their own clumsy embraces during their honeymoon in the strange Western-style hotel at Miyazaki in Kyushu, whose palm trees provided a romantic background for so many in the days when flights to Guam, Hawaii or even Okinawa were undreamt of by ordinary people.

"A maid would also know when the young woman had her periods, and would probably notice when she missed

123

one. But what I don't see," Hanae continued, "is what all this has to do with an attempt to kill the British Ambassador." Although by no means restored to her normal equable manner, she seemed willing to discuss the matter in a reasonable way.

"Nothing at all," Otani said, suddenly remembering what Ambassador Atsugi of the Foreign Ministry had said to him during their conversation on the campus of Kobe University. Something about the Kyoto police muddying the waters by questioning the Grand Master's family. Had Atsugi by any chance known something?

"No. It's just an idea I'm playing with. Beginning with me we've all just assumed that the bullet was meant for the ambassador. But supposing it was always *intended* to kill the Iemoto. I'm just trying to think around possible motives. Wasting my time, probably."

Hanae actually smiled. It made Otani feel much better. "It's a very fanciful idea. Why on earth should anyone want to murder the poor man?" Even as she spoke, she shivered a little at the recollection of the unmistakable sexual message in the Grand Master's eyes as they had met hers briefly a few minutes before his death; and reflected that a jealous woman might well be driven to extremes by such a man.

"I don't know," her husband replied. "Money, perhaps? The Southern School must be incredibly wealthy." He made a mental note to consult a knowledgeable fellow Rotarian about the matter. "You know the system of licensing as well as I do, with all these traditional arts. A part of every fee paid by every one of the hundreds of thousands of girls all over the country learning the tea ceremony from a licensed Southern School teacher finds its way to the centre, doesn't it? That's big money, quite apart from the fees the Grand Master collects directly. Think of all the money people like us handed over as gifts for the privilege of going to the New Year tea ceremony, for a

124

start. I rather doubt if the tax authorities will hear much about it.''

Otani sat back, quite carried away by his own eloquence. "Just think about it. What would a young girl's family have to pay each month for a weekly lesson? Five, ten thousand yen? For a six-month course. Say fifty thousand in round figures. And suppose ten or even five per cent of that goes to Kyoto headquarters? A *minimum* of two or three thousand yen for every single student, and there are literally hundreds of thousands at any given time, right? Why, that's tens of millions of yen a year. An office worker, say a middle manager, earns perhaps four million.''

Hanae's eyes widened. "I hadn't thought of it like that. Of course, it must be frightfully expensive to keep that place going. And the women of the family couldn't allow themselves to be seen in anything but the most expensive kimonos, and so on . . .'' Her voice trailed away into silence as she tried to visualise the possible scale of the income accruing to the Southern School and at the absolute disposal of its Grand Master.

Otani too was lost in speculation, trying to work out possible motives for murdering the Grand Master. The son who had succeeded him would, on this hypothesis, be a prime suspect, since the school's vast revenues would now go straight to him. Yet he might simply be a channel through which money could pass to someone who had some kind of hold over him. Was it conceivable that Fujiwara as the putative father of the new head of the school needed money so badly that he had plotted the death of his predecessor, a vigorous man who might well have lived another twenty years in the normal course of events?

His thoughts were interrupted by the shrilling of the telephone. He got up and went to it at once, shaking his head to try to clear his mind. It was Kimura, calling from his flat. "Chief? I've just had Inspector Mihara on the line

125

from Kyoto. He wanted to speak to you, but the duty officer didn't want to disturb you and put him on to me instead. As a matter of fact, I was on the point of going out." As he added these words in a pained manner Kimura looked anxiously at the electric clock in his tiny kitchen, the only timepiece he possessed which was reasonably reliable. He was going to be late for a date with the new secretary in the British Consulate General. It had needed patience and dedication to set it up, and Kimura hoped very much that she wouldn't have given him up as a bad job by the time he arrived at the bar in the basement of the Oriental Hotel.

Otani sighed heavily. "The sooner you tell me what he said, the sooner you can go and meet her, Kimura-kun."

"Meet who? Oh. Well, as a matter of fact . . . oh, well. What he said was rather surprising. It seems that Fujiwara has already shuffled his staff. He's put Sakamoto in charge of the criminal investigation section up there in Kyoto. And Sakamoto has arrested the young Irishman, Casey."

"WHAT?"

"Yes, on suspicion of attempted murder of the British Ambassador, and the manslaughter of the late Grand Master. And there's more. Look, Chief, I shall have to hurry, but perhaps you'd better ring Mihara yourself, at his home. I have the number. Mihara told me this in confidence, but he thinks that Fujiwara will be transferring him to other duties, and that we shall have to liaise with Sakamoto over all this business from tomorrow onwards."

Chapter 16

THE FOLLOWING DAY WAS ONE OF CONFUSION AND FRUS-
tration and by mid-afternoon Otani felt very tired, and
heartily sick of the whole business. It was as Kimura had
said and Inspector Mihara confirmed when Otani telephoned him the same evening. Otani was by no means a
stickler for prescribed procedures and had no compunction
about operating behind Fujiwara's back; especially in the
light of his growing conviction that the commander of the
Kyoto Prefectural Police was involved in the case in some
personal and, at the very least, highly equivocal way. Even
after having been removed from his job as head of the
External Affairs Section of the Kyoto Force, Mihara could
be a valuable ally, and Otani sensed his willingness to help.
Nevertheless, continuing involvement in the affair after formal transfer to other duties could spell serious trouble for
Mihara, and Otani had no wish to be instrumental in dam-
aging the career of an obviously able and intelligent young
officer.

Sakamoto had been on the phone first thing that morning
to Otani, to inform him in the most correct fashion imag-

inable of Casey's arrest. It was as though he had never been a member of Otani's own staff. He identified himself formally as "Inspector Sakamoto, Head of the Criminal Investigation Section, Kyoto Prefectural Police," addressed Otani as though he had been a complete stranger, and announced that he had been assigned by Superintendent Fujiwara to act as liaison officer in place of Inspector Mihara. Otani was requested to deal in future exclusively with Sakamoto in all matters relating to the attempt on the life of the British Ambassador.

The chill unhelpfulness of Sakamoto's tone over the telephone was nothing new to Otani, but as they talked he wished he could have seen his former subordinate's face to judge whether the curious combination of satisfaction and uneasiness he thought he could detect behind the formal phrases was really there, or whether he was just imagining it. Otani had no alternative but to play Sakamoto at his own game, and he replied with equal bureaucratic care in his choice of words. It was quite clear that Fujiwara and Sakamoto between them were trying, in no very subtle fashion, to squeeze him out of the action. Otani for his part had no intention of allowing them to succeed.

He therefore enquired as to the nature of the evidence which had come to Sakamoto's attention and which was of sufficient weight to justify the arrest of the young foreigner, and whether the Irish Embassy in Tokyo had been informed. During the silence which ensued from Sakamoto's end, Otani helpfully mentioned that he understood that in certain consular matters the British authorities had a friendly arrangement by which they acted in cases involving Irish citizens in western Japan, where there was no Irish Consulate as such.

Having had time to think about Otani's questions, Sakamoto proposed a meeting in Kyoto. He added that he was confident that Patrick Casey would in a matter of hours sign a full statement admitting his involvement in the affair and that, needless to say, all the prescribed procedures for cases involving the arrest of foreign nationals would be scrupulously observed.

Although the journey from Kobe to Kyoto was not particularly difficult or time-consuming, Otani had no wish to make it again so soon, so in concluding his conversation with Sakamoto merely indicated that he would make contact with him in due course. He then rang off and at once telephoned Ambassador Atsugi in Osaka.

At least he tried to telephone him, but was told that the ambassador was out of the office. Leaving a message requesting him to call back, Otani replaced the receiver and sat back, rubbing his eyes. In a sense it was just as well. What, after all, could he ask of Atsugi? He could hardly share with him at that stage his half-formed suspicions of Superintendent Fujiwara, based as they were on nothing more than an interesting monologue by a Kyoto innkeeper dredged up by Noguchi following enquiries among his contacts in the considerable underworld of that city; and the odd coincidence of Sakamoto's precipitate departure from his staff and equally sudden reappearance on Fujiwara's.

Yet the latter chain of events was susceptible of a perfectly innocent explanation. Otani himself acknowledged that Sakamoto's complaints about his treatment as one of his senior staff had some justification. His request for a transfer was not in itself unusual in the circumstances, nor his desire to be off at once; and Otani had agreed readily enough. What could be more reasonable than that Sakamoto should wish, after years of being kept at arm's length by Otani and of abrasive relationships with both Noguchi and Kimura, to put himself under the command of a senior officer with whom he had served during the war and who offered him a warm welcome? And finally, what more logical duties for Superintendent Fujiwara to assign to the experienced former head of criminal investigation work in the huge Hyogo police force than similar responsibilities in

129

Kyoto prefecture? Objectively, Otani could see quite well that his line of thinking had very little to support it, and that he had not nearly enough to justify him in a frontal approach involving higher authority.

On the other hand, he was in no way inhibited from sharing his thoughts with his two most trusted associates, and therefore summoned Noguchi and Kimura to a long working lunch in his office, with food brought in from a nearby restaurant. Although Otani had to some extent succeeded in wooing Hanae away from her censorious attitude towards his treatment of Rosie, he had judged it wise to suggest to her that morning that since his movements were uncertain it would probably be better if he went to work without his usual lunch-box.

It had been a useful session, if only in establishing what Kimura and Noguchi themselves thought about Otani's theories, what action they had been taking, and what they suggested should be done in the new situation. Aware of his own tendency to drift away from the point in such discussions, Otani prepared a simple agenda in note form, and stuck to it, making additional notes as they went on.

They began again from the beginning, with Otani describing again the layout of the room and the sequence of events up till the collapse of the Grand Master. Kimura now had a list of the names of all the guests at the fatal tea ceremony, and Otani from his own recollection was able to complete what he thought was an accurate chart of their positions round the walls of the room, which he undertook to check with Hanae later.

Kimura also provided a list of names of all the staff and helpers associated with the school who were present on the Sunday in question, with brief indications of the nature of their duties. They agreed that the people of interest were those who at one time or another were actually inside the room, and one or two whose duties might have taken them into the grounds of the complex of buildings. It was Kimura who suggested that Noguchi would be the right person to talk to the banto, the elderly man whose task it was to deal with the footwear of the guests on arrival and departure, and pointed out that there would be bound to be a gardener on the staff. Although he might well have been off duty as it was a Sunday, he might have noticed if any stranger in the previous few days had shown particular interest in the bamboo grove. Otani thought this a good idea, and even Noguchi grunted approval.

Then they turned to discussion of the necessity for an accomplice inside the premises, and of the apparently insuperable difficulty of ensuring that the British Ambassador would take a prearranged place. Remembering the confusion as the guests had entered the room, the polite but none the less determined battle over precedence and the way in which it was finally settled, Otani felt increasingly dubious about his original idea that the real target had been Sir Rodney Hurtling. He stressed that the only person in the room whose precise position was ordained from the beginning was the Grand Master, whose every movement was prescribed by the ancient ritual.

Noguchi acknowledged the force of Otani's argument, but was not convinced, pointing out that according to Otani's sketch-plan, the ambassador was placed in a direct line between the concealed gunman and the Grand Master. With a surprisingly delicate sense of the rules of Japanese etiquette, he theorised that there were only two possible places where the British Ambassador might have ended up. One was that of the guest of honour, which the diplomat might himself consider he was entitled to, but which it would have been highly improper for him to take in the presence of the Governor of Kyoto Prefecture, who was without question the most senior Japanese guest at this most Japanese of cultural occasions. The other was the place immediately facing the Grand Master, which Japanese guests

131

would unconsciously avoid yet would be entirely appropriate for the distinguished foreigner.

Otani himself was beguiled by this theory, and began to consider the subtlety of an arrangement whereby in the event of the successful assassination of the ambassador investigators might assume that the Grand Master had in fact been the target. They then became mired in consideration of terrorist tactics about which none of them knew enough. Kimura pointed out that the threatening letter delivered to the ambassador in his hotel in Kobe in effect "claimed responsibility", in the grisly phrase familiar to them all from the almost daily reports in the newspapers and on the TV news of outrages of one kind and another committed all over the world in the name of some political or religious cause.

Noguchi was less impressed by the Kobe letter, which had yielded no fingerprints and which he argued was couched in terms so general as to have been capable of being put together by anybody, unlike the others which Kimura had gathered from the ambassador were specific and indicated detailed knowledge of particular events in Northern Ireland. His theory was that it had been a spur-of-the-moment job, a malicious hoax on the part of someone who knew the ambassador had been present when the Grand Master was killed.

Judging by what Kimura had told them of the man's character, it seemed highly probable that he was unpopular with his staff, one of whom might have taken it into his head to frighten him with a macabre joke. Noguchi recommended Kimura to see if he could find out whether anyone on the staff of the British Consulate General in Osaka might have a grievance.

The arrest of Patrick Casey was obviously an event of the greatest possible significance, and they all agreed that if Sakamoto were allowed a free hand it was entirely possible that the young man would make a confession, whether or not he had in fact been implicated. Confessions were after all by far the most common means to a conviction in Japan and it was no secret that a high percentage of them were confessions of convenience. Rank and file gangsters were often assigned to take the rap for colleagues in the same organisation, while even people outside the colourful battalions of organised crime who tangled with the law frequently volunteered false confessions in order to protect another member of the family or a close friend.

Not a great deal could be done about this, given the desire on both sides to settle disagreeable matters like crime and punishment with as little fuss as possible. There were also inducements, however, as Otani and his colleagues knew quite well, and which might well persuade someone like Patrick Casey that the simplest way out of his predicament would be to put his seal—or in the Irishman's case his signature and thumbprint—to a cock and bull story.

In the quiet of Otani's big, shabby office, the three men pondered Sakamoto's action for a long time, concluding that he must have come upon some incontrovertible evidence of Casey's guilt, or be very confident of his ability to extract a confession from the young man.

"There is another possibility," Otani said before turning to the next item on his simple agenda, which was to agree with Kimura and Noguchi on the action each of them would be taking before their next conference. "And that is, that Fujiwara has ordered Sakamoto to make the arrest in order to divert attention away from the Minamikuni family. That would indicate that he might go to extreme lengths to settle the case his way." He looked at Kimura. "I want to make quite sure that Casey's Embassy is notified of his confinement, Kimura, and I want you to come with me to interview the young man. He speaks good Japanese, but I want you to talk to him in English."

He paused for some time and drank a cup of green tea before continuing. "Ninja, I'd like you to do what you can through your contacts to check what happened to that woman's baby. The innkeeper, I mean. At this stage I'd like to avoid a direct approach to the local ward office in Kyoto for a copy of her family register. Her nephew would have the answer, I expect.'' Noguchi, who was picking his teeth, nodded off-handedly, and Otani sat back in his chair and gazed at the dingy ceiling.

"I also want to know more about the Minamikuni family generally. Kimura-kun, you can help there. Again, I think it would be better to by-pass the obvious routes. This young woman you met . . . the one who works in the office there . . .''

Kimura beamed eagerly at the upturned chin of his superior. "Mie Nakazato, her name is, Chief. A very intelligent girl.''

"I'll take your word for it. I hope she is, anyway. Is she also discreet, do you think?''

"I think she'll co-operate, Chief.'' Kimura closed his eyes momentarily to enjoy a fleeting daydream involving Mie Nakazato's co-operation.

"Well, we must take a chance. She would seem to be the best potential source of information apart from Mrs Uemura at the inn, and we already know that Mrs Uemura is a person the new Iemoto confides in. I'd rather not press her too far. As it is, the Iemoto has almost certainly been told by her about our interest in Fujiwara.'' Otani's head had reverted to its normal position, and he stared round at his colleagues, his eyes wide and bright. "I wonder if he knows everything she told Ninja and me? I'd give a lot to know. Anyway, Kimura, you'd better arrange to meet this young woman privately somewhere. Get all you can from her about the Grand Master's mother. Her relationship with her late husband . . . also about the new Iemoto. How did he get on with his father, money matters, that sort of thing. And do try to impress on her that she should keep her mouth shut, will you?''

Kimura took a deep breath. He could not recall the last time Otani had actually *instructed* him to arrange a clandestine meeting with an attractive girl and worm his way into her confidence.

"Yes, sir!" he said fervently, avoiding Ninja Noguchi's eye.

Chapter 17

EVERY POSSIBLE OBSTACLE WAS PUT IN THE WAY OF Otani's expressed wish to interview Patrick Casey in the company of Kimura, or even for that matter on his own, though Sakamoto did make much of the fact that Casey had an excellent command of the Japanese language. Choosing his words with the greatest of care, Otani therefore leant on Sakamoto very heavily. He first stressed the fact that he, Otani, had been formally assigned by the Superintendent-General of the National Police Agency to co-ordinate the investigation, and that Superintendent Fujiwara as commander of the Kyoto force had received written orders to co-operate.

Then Otani mentioned the double interest which the Foreign Ministry had in the affair; both because of the presumption that there had been an attempt on the life of the British Ambassador, and now because a foreigner had been formally charged with complicity. Otani had not in fact yet heard from Atsugi of the Foreign Ministry Liaison Office in Osaka, but had every intention when he did of reporting the arrest of Casey and asking Atsugi to ensure that the

Irish Ambassador in person was summoned to the Ministry in Tokyo to discuss its implications.

Otani asked Sakamoto again whether steps had been taken to notify the Irish authorities and when Sakamoto prevaricated, inferred that they had not. When Otani offered to take the problem up directly with the National Police Agency in Tokyo unless Superintendent Fujiwara would prefer to discuss it with him direct, Sakamoto eventually capitulated and an appointment was made for Otani and Kimura to interview Casey the following morning at 9.30.

After ringing through to Kimura and arranging to meet him the next morning at the Northern Divisional Police Headquarters in Kyoto where Casey was being held, Otani thought carefully before making his next call, which was to Inspector Mihara's home number. He did not expect to find him there, but Mrs Mihara who answered sounded like a sensible and understanding sort of person. Even so, Otani did not identify himself fully to her, merely giving his name and asking her to be kind enough to ask her husband to ring him either at work or at home, depending on the time, and yes, he knew the numbers. It seemed that Mihara might not be back till quite late in the evening, but would be telephoning her earlier.

Otani rang off, hoping very much that he would and that he would be able to speak to Mihara before the end of the day. He told himself that he was being foolish, that deaths in police custody were nowadays unheard of, and that however anxious he might be to divert attention from the Minamikuni family, Fujiwara would neither contemplate, nor be able to bring about, any attempt to silence Casey while making it look like an admission of guilt on his part. All the same, he knew that he would be relieved to see the young man the next day, and thought back briefly to the good impression Casey had made on him, even allowing for the bizarre notion of the very existence of an Irish master of the tea ceremony.

It was an afternoon for almost continuous activity on the telephone. Otani was just about to put the notes of his conference with Noguchi and Kimura into some sort of order when Hanae telephoned; a thing she hardly ever did. She sounded quite restored to her normal peaceable self, and there was a hesitancy about her apology for disturbing him which gentled Otani's whole mood. What Hanae had to tell him was reassuring, too. A parcel had just been delivered at the Otani house from the natural foods department of a big store in Nagoya, a present to them both from Rosie. There had also been a letter from her in the post, written in what Hanae said was very odd Japanese, amounting to an apology for her abrupt departure. Rosie was now at Nanzan University for her special course, and hoped to see the Otanis again before her return to England.

It was good news to Otani, not only because it signalled that hostilities with Hanae were at an end, but also that his uneasy surmise that Rosie might herself be mixed up in some way with the Kyoto murder now seemed to have been pure fantasy. He had long ago learned from her with some surprise that there were probably no more than a few dozen university students of Japanese at any one time in the whole of Britain, so it was not really in the least surprising that she should be acquainted with a recent graduate of her own college.

Otani was less gratified when Hanae told him what was in the parcel. Yet more brown rice, it seemed, of a processed variety which it was claimed on the package could be cooked in the same convenient way as white rice; various packages of seeds and lentils, a jar of honey and some shampoo which was imported from America and appeared to have been made from beans of some kind. Still, he agreed with Hanae that it represented a kindly thought on Rosie's part and a significant blow to her modest budget,

138

and rang off contentedly enough to reflect for a minute on the feasibility of taking Hanae to Nagoya on the bullet-train the following Sunday in order to call on Rosie and entertain her in some way.

He was not left in peace for very long before the door was opened and the absence of a preliminary knock enabled Otani to guess before he saw him that Noguchi was paying him a visit. He stood up and stretched as Noguchi made for his usual chair, then went and joined him. "Back already, Ninja? I thought you were off to Kyoto."

Noguchi shook his head. "Later, maybe." Noguchi never had been the most communicative of men, and Otani waited patiently enough as he yawned, inserted a gnarled finger into one ear and then inspected his findings before looking at his superior. "Gunman. Been talking to a friend of mine about that. Rifle, you see. Unusual."

Otani nodded. He always studied the annual reports and statistics relating to seizures of illegal firearms and knew very well that the vast, indeed overwhelming, majority were handguns. "True enough, Ninja," he agreed. "On the other hand, there are plenty of properly licensed sporting rifles around. Most hunters use shotguns, I know, but all the same . . ."

Noguchi reached down and scratched his leg, revealing the dingy white of long woollen underwear as still favoured by many men of his generation during the winter, though Otani himself had not worn it for decades. He puffed a bit as he straightened up, then opened one eye quite wide and peered at Otani. "Not still thinking about that fellow Terada, are you? Guy that Kimura interviewed? Theory about a sportsman cleaning his gun, went off accidentally? Come off it."

Otani tolerated familiarities from both his closest associates, especially Noguchi, which would have been unthinkable from anyone else in his entire circle of acquaintance.

139

Nevertheless, he was nettled by the obvious scorn in Noguchi's voice, and sat back rather stiffly.

"I examined the scene within minutes of the shot, Ninja. Let me remind you of that. I attach no more weight to the suggestion that the administrator Terada made to Kimura than you do. Besides, the house across the alley at the back has been checked. It is owned by a respected professor of Chinese history at Kyoto University. Neither he nor any member of his family possesses a licensed firearm. Quite apart from that, it isn't technically feasible for the shot to have been fired from that house, nor from the storehouse in its garden. My point is that rifles as such are, as a matter of fact, rather easier to come by in Japan than handguns, simply because it's not illegal to own one for hunting purposes."

Noguchi grunted what might have been an apology. "All right. Look at it this way, though. Nobody but a genius could have brought off that killing with an ordinary sporting rifle. Doesn't matter whether he was after the Iemoto or the ambassador. See what I'm driving at?"

Otani shook his head. "No, not really. Are you trying to tell me that a professional gunman brought a high-precision weapon into the country with him? I don't believe it, Ninja. The controls are too good. That sort of thing only happens in television films."

"I'll spell it out. It must have been a sniper's rifle. A sharpshooter's weapon. Right? Who has hardware like that?"

Otani could have kicked himself. "Of *course*! The Ground Self-Defence Forces!" The phrase still sounded unnatural on the lips of people who not only remembered but had as likely as not served in the Imperial Japanese Army, but Noguchi forbore to offer the sort of sardonic comment he usually made when the subject of Japan's modern armed forces cropped up.

"Right. Not impossible, maybe. To pay a trained army
140

sniper for a job like that. Unlikely though. And I agree it would be a hell of a job for a *gaijin* hit-man to bring a rifle into the country.''

''Why is it unlikely that it could have been a GSDF gun?'' Otani had been rather pleased with the theory, and looked with some irritation at Noguchi, who stared back at him unhelpfully.

''Of course it's unlikely. It's not like the war, you know, when they made us take them home on leave with us. Know anything about the sort of controls they have in the services nowadays on the storage and issue of weapons and ammunition?''

Otani shook his head. ''Not really. Very much like our own in the police . . .'' His voice trailed away as it finally dawned on him. ''I'm sorry, Ninja,'' he said then with an embarrassed smile. ''I must be getting senile. It simply never occurred to me. *We* have trained police sharpshooters and a few weapons for them here at headquarters . . .''

Noguchi nodded, and then passed a meaty hand over his bristly hair. ''We have,'' he agreed. ''So does Fujiwara, I dare say.''

Otani stared at him. ''Get on to Forensic right away, Ninja. They haven't even confirmed the calibre of the damned bullet yet.''

Chapter 18

HAVING SURREPTITIOUSLY CHECKED WHILE SHE WAS away that he had more than enough money on him, Kimura beamed and even went to the extreme of rising from his chair as Mie Nakazato returned from her trip to the ladies' room and resumed her place at their table for two in the grill room at the Miyako Hotel. It was by the huge window, and from where they sat they could see the outline of the northern hills black against the sky, and the lights of the city away to the west. It was not only the gentle glow from the red-shaded candle on the table which made her eyes sparkle, Kimura decided. Watching her approach from the other side of the big room he noted her high colour, even though she was perfectly steady on her feet. French wine was alarmingly expensive at the Miyako, but he hoped and believed that Otani would pass the cost of the meal as a legitimate expense.

The waiter hovered nearby. "Some coffee?" Kimura suggested. "And perhaps a cognac . . . or we might move to the bar after coffee." Miss Nakazato nodded, and Kimura interpreted it the way he preferred, dispatching the waiter for coffee only.

"Thank you. It was a very nice dinner. But I must go home soon."

"Really? Why, it's only a little after nine-thirty." The coffee arrived, and she made no reply until the waiter had finished fussing over them and again withdrawn. Then she smiled, rather sadly, Kimura thought.

"After all, you've got what you wanted from me, haven't you?"

Kimura thought quickly, then nodded his head. Mie Nakazato was obviously no fool, and he decided that for once straightforwardness might be the best tactic. "Yes, in a sense. You've been extremely helpful. And I have absolute confidence in your discretion. It would be dishonest on my part to deny that I asked you to meet me here this evening in order to obtain information from you. I'm a police officer, as you well know, and we're in the middle of a very tricky investigation. What you've told me about the Minamikunis is very helpful, and I'm grateful."

To his great surprise a tear welled up at the corner of one eye. Mie Nakazato brushed it away almost angrily. "I wouldn't have told you all that about the sensei if I hadn't been so worried about Casey-san."

"It's what you told me about Mrs Minamikuni's sister that's even more important. I know it must have been difficult for you, believe me." He paused, then risked putting a hand on hers before continuing. She did not withdraw. "But that's not all. This is difficult for *me* to say. You must be able to see . . . I find you very attractive. I was very excited at the prospect of seeing you again. Just personally, I mean. Nothing to do with police business. And I hope we can meet often, after all this is sorted out."

At this the girl's lip curled in a wry smile. "I'm very

143

flattered. But I expect your wife would have something to say about that." It was a point frequently put to Kimura in the course of early negotiations with new female acquaintances, and it always gave him satisfaction to deal with it. He smiled sweetly, and applied some pressure to the unresisting hand under his.

"Maybe she would, if I were married. But I'm not. Never have been."

Miss Nakazato's eyes widened. "Really?" was all that she said. Then and then only she slowly withdrew her hand.

"I know what you're going to say. Most men of my age are married." She nodded.

"And most men, even if they are, have no compunction about having affairs with other women if they can," she said.

Kimura stirred the remains of his coffee with some violence. "Yes. Well, I can see that you must have become rather disillusioned in view of what you've told me about the late Iemoto. His own sister-in-law, too, you said."

The girl nodded, still looking at Kimura in a way that disconcerted him. The discussion was indeed moving smoothly back to the subject of sex, but not in quite the promising way he had envisaged. "Among a great many others." It was time to score a modest point.

"Well, she's a married woman, if it comes to that. It's my belief that women are just as ready to be unfaithful as men. They don't on the whole have as many opportunities, that's all." Kimura was drawing on his own experience, and felt he knew what he was talking about.

A tip of Mie Nakazato's red tongue became visible as she delicately moistened her lower lip, to such erotic effect that Kimura felt himself responding physically, even while thinking that a gin and tonic and half a bottle of wine seemed to have revealed unexpected depths in one he had taken to be an intelligent but basically well-bred, conventional "office lady".

"You may be right," she said. From where they were sitting Kimura could see the neon signs of several "love" hotels in the block between Sanjo Street in which the Miyako Hotel stands and the Nanzenji temple complex half a mile away at the foot of the wooded hills; and he began to wonder whether things might move faster than he had dared to hope.

"All the same, you said that Mrs Minamikuni reacted very strongly when she found out that her husband was having an affair with her sister."

Mie nodded. "Very strongly. I heard from Terada-san that when they were both young Mrs Minamikuni used to really dominate her younger sister. Then when her husband was elected Governor the younger one seemed to enjoy getting her own back. Here in Kyoto at least she's now more important than Mrs Minamikuni. Of course, any time she likes Mrs Minamikuni could wreck the Governor's career, though. She has letters her sister wrote to the sensei, you see. The Governor's political opponents could bring him down easily at the next election by publishing them."

"Let's go to the bar, shall we?" Kimura was reluctant to interrupt the flow, but they were the only diners left and the staff of the grill room were beginning to hover in their vicinity. He need not have worried. Mie made no move to go home and two cognacs later was still happily analysing Mrs Minamikuni's relationship with her younger sister after her elevation to the status of wife of the prefectural governor and her affair with the late Iemoto.

Kimura had matched Mie drink for drink, but prided himself on his head for liquor. He was fascinated by Mie, who seemed to him to have many of the qualities of the Western women he normally sought out, while occasion-

145

ally reverting to the demureness normally characteristic of well-brought-up Japanese girls of her age. He found the combination powerfully attractive especially when she was talking about sex.

"Mrs Minamikuni didn't follow her husband's example, then? You haven't said anything about her having lovers."

Mie laughed. "Well, she is fifty, you know."

"That's not so old," Kimura protested stoutly. As he spoke there flashed into his mind the recollection of a most satisfying episode he had experienced several years beforehand in the company of a lady certainly old enough to be his mother, the wife of a Swiss businessman.

Mie brushed a stray hair from her cheek. "No, you're right. She does take care of herself, and looks a lot less than her age. One day when Terada-san had been drinking he told me that Mrs Minamikuni had really wanted to marry Fujiwara-san and never really cared about her husband or anyone else. Maybe she sees him sometimes, but I don't think she has any lovers apart from him, if he is."

Abruptly she stood up. "It's late. I must go." Something about her manner completely dissipated the lingering hope in the background of Kimura's consciousness of a visit to a love hotel. He was surprised to realise that this rather pleased him than otherwise, even or perhaps especially when Mie brushed past him after he too had stood up and he distinctly felt her warmth and noticed the fragrance of her perfume.

They were silent in the taxi to her home, a solid middle-class house in the Kitashirakawa area not far from Kyoto University, but Kimura sensed that Mie was as aware of their proximity as he was. She bade him a friendly goodnight, once more the self-possessed secretary he had met for the first time only a day or so beforehand, and he got back into the taxi in a thoroughly unsettled frame of mind. It would be frightful if at his age he was actually falling in love.

Chapter 19

"**Y**OU SPEAK AND UNDERSTAND JAPANESE extremely well. I know that, Casey-san. And so I may want to put the occasional question to you myself. All the same I've asked Inspector Kimura here to come along with me and have a talk with you in English. You may feel more comfortable using your own language. All this must be a great strain on you." Otani nodded at the young Irishman and then turned back and watched as the incomprehensible babble of English with its leaps and swoops and alien melodies began. Otani caught a word here and there, of course. So many English words have found their way in more or less garbled form into Japanese that it would have been extraordinary if he hadn't. Nevertheless, it was in one way almost an advantage not to understand what was being said; it sharpened his powers of observation.

Patrick Casey looked pale and tense, as well he might. The first mental note Otani made was to insist when the interview was over that he be permitted the use of an electric razor. The stubble on his face was that of a young man,

148

soft and patchy, but it still made him look much more of a potential criminal than he did clean-shaven. The interview room was bare, furnished only with a table and three upright chairs and, being on the northern side of the building, was chilly, in spite of the old-fashioned radiator burbling and thumping against one wall.

Casey was wearing jeans and a none-too-clean shirt, over which was a pullover rather worn at the elbows, and there were dark patches under his eyes. He did seem to relax just a little as Kimura spoke to him in what seemed to Otani to be a suitably friendly, encouraging way, and the convulsive rubbing of the thumb of his right hand over the four fingertips began to slow down.

". . . so you actually left Ireland a good many years ago," Kimura was saying. "Of course, you went home during the vacations while you were at the University of London, though." Casey nodded. "And then you applied for a Japanese Government Scholarship to come here for two years and were lucky enough to get one."

"That's right," Casey said, and a wan smile illuminated his face briefly. "Not to study the tea ceremony, mind you. I don't think they'd have given me one for that. It was to study Japanese history of the sixteenth century. After language training they fixed up for me to be attached to Kyoto University. Well, I knew a bit about the history of the tea ceremony and how keen Hideyoshi Toyotomi was on it—you know who Hideyoshi was?"

It was like asking an Englishman whether he's ever heard of Henry VIII, and Kimura grinned. "I'm no scholar, Mr Casey, but yes. I do."

"Sorry. Well, I found myself here at the very centre of the tea ceremony tradition, and one of my Japanese professors arranged for me to call on the Grand Master . . . the late Grand Master, you understand. And he was very kind, and, well, before I knew what was happening I was hooked. So when he offered to give me lessons personally,

149

well . . ." He shrugged, and Kimura nodded understandingly.

It was not easy for Kimura. He knew well enough what Otani wanted of him, but no idea what had been said in previous sessions with Sakamoto. "I understand. So you found yourself in the Minamikuni household more or less by accident. All right. Let's turn to recent events. When did you first hear that the British Ambassador would be attending the special New Year ceremony last Sunday?"

"Me? Why, I had no idea until the day itself. I knew there would be a lot of VIPs there . . . and I suppose, let me think, yes, I think somebody said something about some ambassadors while we were making the preparations, but people were more excited about the Governor of Kyoto Prefecture, I believe." Kimura rather hoped he might have an opportunity to convey this information to Sir Rodney Hurtling some time.

"Let me put it another way. I presume the invitations would have been sent out and reply cards received well before the holiday period?" Kimura was certain that this would have been the case, and it would be a simple matter to confirm it with Mie Nakazato. Come to think of it, the Superintendent had himself received one and would remember when.

Casey looked genuinely bewildered. "Why, I suppose so. I have no idea how these things are done."

Otani noticed the expression on the Irishman's face and fired a question at him in Japanese. "Are you interested in politics, Casey-san?" Kimura was irritated by his intervention, but almost automatically began to interpret Otani's words into English, before subsiding as Casey replied in Japanese.

"I've already gone into all that with the other Inspector."

Otani had surmised as much, and merely nodded. He

had wondered on their arrival whether to confront Sakamoto before seeing Casey, but had decided against. A confrontation would be necessary, but he wanted the benefit of Kimura's advice first. Otani had never been able to understand Kimura's taste for the company of *gaijin*, but had the greatest possible respect for his apparently magical insight into their psychological processes.

After an uncertain pause during which Kimura wondered whether Otani intended to say any more, Kimura turned again to Casey. "We know that quite well, Mr Casey," he said in English. "You will very probably be asked the same questions by different police officers a good many more times yet, so you might as well get used to it. The Superintendent and I are particularly interested to know why you went to Kobe this week. You seem to have a knack of showing up wherever the British Ambassador goes."

Otani noted that the friendly tone had disappeared from Kimura's voice, but was not displeased. Casey had been put comparatively at ease at the beginning of the interview, and there were good tactical reasons why they should turn a screw or two at this stage. Casey flushed, whether with anger or embarrassment was not at first obvious, but his subsequent words sounded hot and intemperate to Otani.

"I know what you're getting at, all of you. Holy Mary, there are millions of Irish. How many in the IRA? A few hundred? I neither know nor care who the British Ambassador is or where the terrible man goes or what he does—"

"Why do you call him a 'terrible man', then?" Kimura enquired keenly, and Casey flapped a hand in exasperation.

"Will ye *listen* to me? It's just an Irish expression, doesn't mean a thing. You made me get me rag out

151

and . . ." He ran a shaking hand through his hair, at a loss for words.

Kimura's ear was keen and he had in any case noted the broadening of Casey's Irish accent when he became excited. "All right, calm down. I'm not 'getting at' anything. I just want to know what you were doing in Kobe. You've given a perfectly acceptable explanation of your presence at the tea ceremony in Kyoto, and I'm willing to take your word for it at this stage that you didn't necessarily know that the ambassador was going to be there. On the other hand there was quite a lot of publicity in the Press—including the English language papers—about the European Community Trade Fair opening ceremony in Kobe."

Casey clenched his fists in impotent frustration. "Even if I had gone there for their wretched Trade Fair I wouldn't need to feel apologetic, now would I? Ireland belongs to the Community. And I haven't heard that anybody got killed there." A look of stark horror spread over his face. "My God, *did* somebody get killed?"

Kimura was tempted to let him think so for a while, but could not bring himself to do it. "No, Mr Casey. Nobody was killed."

Casey closed his eyes momentarily, then straightened up and looked at Otani. "Superintendent Otani knows what I was doing in Kobe," he said then. "I went to meet an old friend of mine who was staying with him."

At this point the artificiality of the situation became absurd to Kimura, and he switched to Japanese, turning himself to his superior. "I think we should continue this discussion in Japanese, sir," he said. "Mr Casey has just told me that he was in Kobe merely to meet the young lady you told me you invited from England."

Otani nodded. "That's correct. I ran into them both not far from the Oriental Hotel." He looked at Casey. "I can certainly vouch for that," he said. "Though only you know what your movements were after I left you. I do know that Winchmore-san arrived back at my house in the middle of the night. I also know that you did not return to your hotel that night. Where did you stay, Casey-san?''

A dark flush mantled Patrick Casey's cheeks. "That's a private matter," he muttered.

Otani stiffened and spoke in his most formal manner. "Let me remind you that you are in very serious trouble. You are accused of complicity in a conspiracy to murder, and as an accomplice to manslaughter. Your position could scarcely be worse. Quite apart from that, it is a requirement of the law that foreigners must at all times notify their whereabouts to the authorities. This means that you must either be at your registered address or a registered guest in a hotel. *Where did you spend the night?* Tell the Inspector.''

The colour was now drained from Casey's face as Kimura leaned forward and pressed the attack in English. "Well? You understood what the Superintendent asked. Come on now. Where were you?''

Casey muttered in such a low voice that Kimura had to stop him twice and ask him to speak up. Otherwise neither he nor Otani interrupted. "Rosie Winchmore and I used to—well, when she first started at the university and I was in my final year we . . . we got it together for a few months, until she met the fellow she has now, Roger his name is. Anyway we kept in touch a bit. There was no particular row, you see, and when I came here she used to write now and then. So naturally it was a good chance to meet again when she wrote to say she'd be in Rokko for a few days and then in Nagoya, both not far from Kyoto. That evening. . . well, we walked and talked and then met Mr Otani here . . . then we had a few drinks, and, well, we went to one of those coffee shops with the private rooms, you know?''

Kimura looked at Otani and nodded twice, almost

imperceptibly, in a prearranged code to indicate that he found the Irishman's story convincing. Otani was tempted to bring pressure to bear through the National Police Agency and the Foreign Ministry to have him transferred to Hyogo Police custody, but following his confidential conversation with Inspector Mihara at home the previous evening, was now reasonably confident that no harm would come to Casey. In the meantime it was important for Sakamoto and Fujiwara to think that he was still pursuing his own original idea that an attempt had actually been made to murder the British Ambassador, and that it had resulted instead in the killing of the elder Minamikuni.

"Explain to him, Inspector," he instructed Kimura, and after a quick glance to which Otani responded with a nod, Kimura began to speak in a voluble undertone to Casey in English. Otani could not begin to guess whether or not they were being overheard or the conversation recorded, but had agreed with Kimura on the way that the points he wanted to be made to the young man had better be put in English, and as idiomatically as possible. It was more than likely that Fujiwara or one of his staff other than Mihara understood English, but Otani was prepared to bet that nobody in the Kyoto force could approach anything like Kimura's standard of fluency. Sakamoto, so far as he knew, spoke not a word of the language.

He waited and watched patiently as Kimura rapidly told Casey that his Embassy in Tokyo had been informed of his arrest, and that his interests would be fully protected. That he was undoubtedly under some suspicion of involvement in a criminal conspiracy and at the very least would in all probability be required to give evidence as a material witness. That in the meantime he should answer such factual questions as were put to him by any police officer truthfully, but to offer no opinions and above all to sign no documents, either in Japanese or English, irrespective of

154

whether or not he agreed with their contents. Kimura concluded by saying that he hoped that it would be possible to complete their enquiries within a day or two and urging Casey to try to be patient.

As the expressions of bewilderment and the beginnings of relief chased each other in succession across the young tea master's face, Otani wondered how long he could keep all these plates in the air. It was absolutely vital to secure some hard evidence against Superintendent Fujiwara if he was to proceed against him openly. As matters stood, he had not even enough material to complete the hypothesis he was building up in his own mind; certainly not enough to take to the National Police Agency with a request for an internal enquiry, let alone for a case to be put to the district prosecutor.

There was no particular reluctance to institute criminal proceedings against police officers—there had been a spectacular case not long before involving several members of the Osaka force who had been running their own protection racket—but to accuse a man of Fujiwara's seniority would be a grave matter indeed. Otani hoped with all his heart that the instructions he had given Noguchi, following their conversation about the rifle, would turn out to have been the right ones and that Noguchi would find what Otani hoped he might. It had been more difficult to persuade Atsugi of the Foreign Ministry to do what he had asked of him, but he eventually agreed.

He and Kimura had got as much as they usefully could out of Casey in the inhibiting environment of one of Fujiwara's divisional headquarters, even though the young Irishman would certainly be able to help a lot at a later stage. When they had met that morning outside the building Kimura had obviously been bursting to report on a conversation he had had with Mie Nakazato the previous evening; but that would have to wait a while. The immediate need was to talk to Sakamoto.

155

Chapter 20

"**W**E ACTED UPON INFORMATION RECEIVED, SUPER-intendent." Sakamoto's thin lips closed firmly after the last word, and he fixed his eyes on the meticulously ordered pen-tray in front of him. The office he had been allotted in Kyoto Prefectural Police Headquarters was more spacious than that he had occupied in Kobe, and he had after all had the use of it for only a very short time. Nevertheless its bare emptiness was depressing to Otani.

"I must ask you the nature of the information. You may or may not be aware that the Irish Ambassador has called personally at the Foreign Ministry in Tokyo to express his concern over the arrest of Casey, and has been promised a full report. He will no doubt demand consular access to the young man before long." Sakamoto said nothing, and this came as something of a surprise to Otani. He was used to Sakamoto in complaining moods, or even showing something approaching acidulous satisfaction when reporting on some petty infringement of the police regulations by one of his colleagues, but had never found him uncommunicative before. "I must ask you the nature of the information," he repeated icily.

Sakamoto's gaze remained focused on the orderly pile of paper-clips in their special compartment of the pen-tray. "An anonymous telephone call," he said at last. "To the effect that Casey was the author of the death threat received by the British Ambassador at his hotel in Kobe. To the further effect that evidence of his authorship was to be found in his hotel room in Kyoto. A search was made of his room, and certain articles were found."

Sakamoto pulled open one of the drawers of his desk and took out a folder, which he pushed across to Otani. "You will observe that the newspaper has been mutilated," Sakamoto said as Otani opened it to find a copy of the English-language *Mainichi Daily News* folded to show that parts of one page had been cut out with scissors. He lifted it to find a photocopy of a page of a Japanese-language book which evidently dealt with the history of the tea ceremony. The page in question included a plan of the oldest part of the Southern School headquarters complete with the dimensions of the rooms. The folder also contained a publicity brochure put out by the Kobe International Trade Centre where the European Fair had been opened by the assembled envoys of the European Community. After the manner of its kind, the brochure too incorporated plans of the layout of each floor, with measurements.

"Casey's fingerprints are on each of these items," Sakamoto said thinly. "Do not hesitate to handle them yourself, Superintendent. They have been photographed. I should add that a sample has been taken from the portable typewriter found in Casey's room. I would recommend that it be compared with the typing on the envelope." A ghost of a smile flitted over the death's head face. "You are about to ask me how it comes about that we in Kyoto have any knowledge of the letter in question. There is no mystery,

157

Superintendent. It was the first thing the manager of the hotel mentioned to me when I telephoned him. I had intended it as a mere courtesy enquiry after the ambassador's well-being following his departure from Kyoto Prefecture and the protection of this force. The manager is an old acquaintance of mine and one who was often helpful to me during my years on your staff. He will, I am sure, confirm what I have told you if for any reason you wish to check with him.''

'I have, as you know, been talking to Casey myself this morning,'' Otani said as equably as he could, thinking furiously. ''I too made it quite clear to him that he is under suspicion. This . . . this *evidence* you have produced is hardly conclusive, however.'' He pushed the folder aside contemptuously.

''He is manifestly guilty.'' Sakamoto rapped out the words angrily, and for almost the first time stared Otani full in the face. There were spots of red at each cheekbone, and Otani could see a vein throbbing at his temple where the thinning hair had been cropped away to near-baldness.

''That remains to be proved,'' Otani said. ''I take it that Superintendent Fujiwara authorised the action you have taken?''

Sakamoto's eyes glittered. ''Of course. In fact your question is otiose. The Commander has confidence in me. A very different situation from that which prevailed—''

''That's enough, Sakamoto!'' Otani's anger arose and subsided very quickly, but his words acted like a slap on the face to Sakamoto who jerked back swiftly in his chair and clamped his lips together again.

Otani rose to his feet and stared down at his former subordinate. ''I will say only one thing to you about this affair,'' he said. His voice was now controlled, but cold and hard. ''The District Prosecutor will be advised by the Ministry of Justice to examine the case you will be

158

making to him with the utmost care. I remain in charge of this investigation, Inspector, and you will submit the papers to me before they go to the prosecutor.'' The sound of Sakamoto picking up the telephone was quite audible as Otani closed the door behind him without looking back.

Kimura was not waiting at the appointed spot, which was the wooden bridge in the Chinese style which spans the ornamental lake in the middle of the spacious and beautiful garden behind the vermilion, green and white splendour of the Heian Shrine, so Otani put a few coins in the box provided and taking one of the brittle powdery breadsticks leant over the rail, breaking bits off and tossing them to the huge, multicoloured carp which congregated near the bridge waiting for just such treats. The sunshine was still bright, and the fish had not yet entered the comatose state in which they would pass the hardest weeks of winter. They were sluggish, though, and the jostling for the food was less greedy than Otani remembered from previous visits to the shrine in warmer months.

He was tired and worried, but a feeling of affection came over him as he spotted Kimura from some distance away, approaching the bridge with his habitual jaunty swagger. After his session with Sakamoto it was like getting out of a suit and necktie and putting on a comfortable yukata. Kimura grinned as he eventually caught Otani's eye and quickened his pace, only to stop almost at once and survey with an air of extravagant admiration two girls who had briefly strayed from a party of high-school pupils being conducted round the garden by a girl bus guide in a powder-blue uniform who was holding in one white-gloved hand a small flag with the number 5 on it. Although their navy-blue sailor-style tops and overlong voluminous pleated skirts were dismally unbecoming, the girls were quite pretty.

"Come, come, Kimura," Otani said as he finally approached. "If you'd married at the proper time, you'd probably have a daughter of their age. You should be ashamed of yourself. Well, out with it, man! We can talk about this morning afterwards. What about this secretary you saw last night?" He passed Kimura a chunk of the breadstick and between them they soon distributed the remainder of it to the seemingly bored carp. Otani had long since given up any serious attempt to get Kimura married off, but Kimura was still distinctly shaken by the impact of Mie Nakazato, and looked warily at his superior before he replied, choosing his words with care.

"Yes. She was very helpful—within limits, of course. After all, she is only a secretary, but in a job like that she could hardly help finding out a good deal about the family situation. Sorry I'm a bit late . . . to tell you the truth, I was on the phone to her. Just checking one or two points."

Otani looked at him quizzically, but made no comment, and after a moment Kimura began again. "You know, the late lamented Iemoto really was an amazing old goat." The note of jealous admiration in Kimura's voice was very obvious, and he moved a little closer to Otani. "Dozens of them, and his wife didn't seem to bother in the least." A disturbing thought struck Kimura. "I can't believe he would ever have tried it with Nakazato-san herself, though," he added stoutly, but with a slight frown. "That is to say, his wife turned a blind eye except when he had an affair with her own younger sister. Who just happens to be the Governor's wife."

Otani straightened up very slowly and brushed the crumbs off his hands. "Indeed? That's extremely interesting." His voice sounded very quiet and far away, and Kimura preened himself. "I thought you'd find that bit of background useful. Yes, apparently the fur really flew, but in that special Kyoto way—you know, vicious but quiet."

160

"Yes, yes, I see," Otani said absently, leaving Kimura in some doubt whether he had taken in what he had just said. "Let's take a stroll round the lake, Kimura."

They set off, but for some time Otani said nothing more, and Kimura began to find his silence oppressive. "How did you get on with Sakamoto, Chief?" he enquired, and Otani with an apparent effort dragged himself back to his surroundings.

"What? Oh. Sakamoto. Yes." A look of indignation replaced his meditative expression. "They're setting that young fellow up, Kimura-kun. Sakamoto could see I didn't believe a word of what he told me, and scarcely even bothered to pretend. It's absolutely disgraceful. They planted a heap of pathetic so-called 'evidence' in Casey's hotel room and then confronted him with it so that he would handle it and leave prints. Fujiwara or Sakamoto typed that envelope. I'm convinced."

"What envelope?"

"The anonymous note delivered to the British Ambassador in Kobe, of course. I must have been mad to fall for that theory so easily right at the beginning—why, I even suggested it, confound it."

They reached the end of the bridge and began to walk along the paths among the patches of moss, stunted pines and the azalea bushes which would be covered with hot pinks and reds in May. "We need some more pieces to put together, Kimura, and there isn't a lot of time. You really did agree with me about Casey?"

Kimura nodded vigorously. "Definitely. I'd bet my midsummer bonus against a hundred yen that that man's no terrorist. But there's still the question of the gunman, Chief. He was real enough. At least, the bullet was."

"After I'd finished with Sakamoto I went to prefectural headquarters to try to see Fujiwara again," Otani said. "I wanted to find out just what he thought they were playing at. He wasn't there, though. Some sort of check-up at the hospital, they said. I'm inclined to think it's one of those diplomatic illnesses. It's more convenient for him to be out of the way at the moment.'' He stopped suddenly, his shoe scuffing the loose gravel of the path. ''So the Governor's wife is the widow's sister. She was there that Sunday, you know. With her husband.''

Kimura smiled sunnily. ''Come on, Chief. You're not suggesting it was Mrs Minamikuni out there, aiming at her sister, are you? Creeping round the bamboos in her kimono and killing her husband by mistake?''

Otani brushed Kimura's words away with a gesture, not bothering to be irritated with him. He was preoccupied again, visualising the room with its sweet, open-air smell of fresh tatami mats, the natural light softened and subdued by being filtered through the translucent shoji paper, and trying to see again in his mind's eye the woman at the Governor's side. It was no good: he would have to ask Hanae. He had hardly noticed the Governor's lady at the time, except to form an impression that she must be a good bit younger than her husband.

''What about the bank accounts?'' Otani snapped out of his reverie and fired the question abruptly at Kimura.

''Ah. The financial arrangements there are quite interesting. Mrs Minamikuni senior is the authorised signatory for what Nakazato-san called the 'staff account'. In other words, payments of salaries for the permanent staff. That consists of Terada the administrator, Nakazato-san, the old banto who takes care of the shoes and acts as nightwatchman, and the maids.''

''Is that all? I got the impression that there were dozens of people about the place.''

''There are, usually. But they're all pupils or teachers. Good-looking, too, some of those girls. Not only do they help around the place, but quite a few used to get recruited as playmates for the Iemoto. And they paid for the privilege, would you believe it? Anyway, Mrs Mina-

162

mikuni deals with all payments of that kind as well as gardeners' fees, caterers' and florists' bills, electricity, gas and all the routine things. Logical enough, because apparently she's always there, whereas the Grand Master has to do a lot of travelling. I don't know whether the young Mrs Minamikuni will take over all that side of things, now. She's a very colourless creature, according to Nakazato-san.''

"I'm more interested in the school's income, Kimura.''

"I know. But I didn't find out much about that. The fees from teachers all over the country are remitted by bank transfer to the Grand Master's various personal accounts. Presumably his widow will have some claim on them. For at least the past five years all the account books covering revenue have been kept personally by the Grand Master's son—the new Iemoto, I mean. And he prepares the tax returns and so on. Nakazato-san has never seen those books. The only revenue that she and Terada have anything to do with is cash that comes in. An astonishing amount, at that. Apparently practically every guest who ever goes to the place hands over a gift envelope on arrival. Occasions like the New Year ceremonies net more than you and I earn in a month between us. Terada and Miss Nakazato receive the cash and hand it over later to the Grand Master.''

They were nearing the exit to the garden, and soon passed out through the gate and on to the wide expanse of the outer precinct of the shrine. The party of high-school pupils were having a group photograph taken, their guide smiling graciously in their midst, though the expressions on the youngsters' faces were for the most part solemn.

"So there'd be some record of cash receipts,'' Otani said after a lengthy period of rumination.

"Not a bit of it, Chief. No record, no tax, is the way I see it. Although she doesn't trust me enough to say so, I would guess that the Nakazato girl and Terada get useful cash bonuses from time to time as a reward for their reliability.'' In referring to Mie in this dismissive way, Kimura tripped over his tongue, and coughed to cover his confusion.

Otani merely nodded as he paced on, scarcely noticing the parked sightseeing buses outside, the enormous vermilion uprights of the outer *torii* gateway with its great crossbeam, or even the hazy green of the hills to their left. ''Who benefits, Kimura? That's the first and most important question in a murder investigation. The new Grand Master, obviously. He gets status, and complete control of the family income from now on. You talked to him, Kimura. What did you really make of him?''

''Well, he certainly didn't seem to be in the depths of depression. Very smooth, very much in control . . . but quite helpful. Of course, he was very actively involved previously in running things, and now it seems he handled all the trickier side of the finances anyway.''

''Could he be the type to be under his mother's thumb, do you think? Sooner or later I shall have to ask to see the lady. The funeral's tomorrow, isn't it? I can't make up my mind whether to go myself or ask you to.''

Kimura wasn't sure which question to answer first. ''Yes. I mean, no. He doesn't strike me as much of a mother's boy. The funeral is tomorrow, eleven o'clock. It'll be a huge affair. This is the public one, of course. The family ceremony and cremation happened yesterday. They're holding it in the Kyoto Kaikan, just over there.'' Kimura pointed at the grey concrete bulk of the municipal assembly hall on the other side of Okazaki Park. ''Not a lot of point in going, I would have thought, unless you just want to get a look at the family.''

''Fujiwara will go, I presume, but then he'd be expected to anyway in the case of the funeral of such a prominent citizen,'' Otani said. ''I wish I could work out how he benefits from Minamikuni's death.''

"Well, it's a long shot, but his name cropped up last night, too," Kimura said. His further account of his meeting with Mie Nakazato, suitably edited, occupied the rest of the walk to the terminus of the Hankyu Electric Railway from which they took the fast train to Kobe.

Chapter 21

OTANI SAT AT HIS DESK. HE HAD SPENT SO MUCH TIME away from it during the week that routine paperwork had piled up to a daunting extent, so he had given strict orders that he was not to be disturbed for the remainder of the afternoon, and was doggedly going through the heap. Two folders at his side held a special fascination for him, though, and from time to time he turned to them and glanced once more at the papers in them. One was the personnel file of Inspector Masao Sakamoto; the other contained the duty rosters for the past few weeks. It was still surmise, though. Only if Noguchi came back with the information he was still waiting for would Otani feel confident enough to set in train the action he had planned.

In the meantime there were pressing enough problems to occupy him, not least among which was the necessity to find a successor to Sakamoto as head of the Criminal Investigation Section. Otani was far from anxious to bring in a complete stranger to handle the job, which had to be filled by a substantive Inspector. Better, he thought, to consider carefully some of the younger men in charge of divisions up and down the vast, sprawling area of his territory. The Hyogo force was, after all, the third largest in the country, and if the Agency wanted to foist people from Nagasaki on to him, Otani felt that they should be assigned to the periphery and show their paces there before being admitted to his inner council. He sighed. Noguchi would have some useful ideas, he always did.

Try as he would, it was difficult for Otani to give his full attention to many of the reports in the pile before him, and in one case he had moistened his ivory seal with the two Chinese characters for "Otani" on the tiny red pad incorporated in its little leather case and pressed it in approval of a request without having the least idea of what it was. It was therefore with only a show of irritation that he picked up the receiver when the telephone rang. "I thought I had given instructions—" he began, but the operator cut in before he was fairly started.

"Sir, I'm extremely sorry, sir. But there is a lady at the main entrance who insists on seeing you. She has been told that you are occupied on most urgent business, but won't be moved, sir."

"I see. Who is it?"

"That's the problem, sir. She won't say. She seems to be, ah, a very *important* sort of lady." It was very rare indeed for Otani to have any but official visitors, and he was intrigued. The lady must be, if not important, a person with considerable force of character to have induced the officer at the reception desk to pass her request on.

"She's not crazy, is she?"

The voice at the other end sounded shocked. "Oh no, sir. We'd never trouble you with one of those." There was a well-established drill for dealing with the odd-balls who turned up at frequent intervals to report plots to kill the Emperor or the sighting of a flying saucer.

"All right, I'll see her. Have her escorted up." Otani stood up after putting the phone down, stretched and took off his glasses. He needed them for reading, but preferred to do without when in conversation. He crossed to the door and opened it, leaving it wide, and then waited in the centre of the room.

It was quite true. The woman who swept in was quite obviously a person of consequence, and the young officer escorting her looked relieved when Otani dismissed him courteously before bowing to his visitor, who closed the door firmly on her retreating escort before approaching Otani and responding to his bow. The lady was in a black mourning kimono which to Otani's admittedly inexpert eye looked extremely expensive from the appearance of the matt heavy silk. Her hair was immaculate in formal Japanese style and although Otani's visitor was obviously in her middle years her use of make-up was of the type and expertise usually associated with much younger women.

Along with many another Japanese male, Otani was relatively unmoved by beauty in young women, being much more susceptible to *onnazakari*, that remarkable blooming which comes upon many Japanese women around the age of forty, when they put on a little weight, their skin is firm and rosy, and they not infrequently acquire a certain look in the eye. This woman had just such a look, even though there was evidence of anxiety in her face, along with a determination to conceal it from him.

Physically the woman looked a little like his own wife, Hanae, who was herself still very much in this kind of bloom, with Otani deeply thankful for the fact.

"You are welcome," he said gravely. "My name is Otani. I shall be pleased if I can be of assistance to you." He began to fumble for one of his official name-cards, but then thought better of it, being unsure whether middle-aged ladies customarily carried them. Hanae certainly didn't.

"I am sorry to disturb you," his visitor said, not looking at all as if she meant it. "I am Minamikuni." It was a possibility which had flashed through Otani's mind while

168

he was waiting for her to come up, so he was not greatly surprised and in any case never had any trouble in maintaining the poker face for which he was locally famous.

"I am honoured that you should make a troublesome journey to come to see me at such a distressing time. I take it that you are . . ." He let the words hang delicately in the air between them.

"Yes. I am the widow of the late Iemoto."

"Please accept my sincere condolences on your tragic bereavement." Otani indicated the easy-chairs round the low table. "Please be seated." Mrs Minamikuni took the chair normally occupied by Kimura during conferences with Otani, while he settled into his own accustomed seat and studied the new widow's face. Kimura had reported that the lady's son had not seemed greatly distressed by the death of the former Grand Master: it seemed that his widow also was bearing her loss with considerable fortitude.

"Superintendent Otani. I do not wish to trespass unduly on your time," she began after arranging herself with some style in Kimura's chair. "I understand that you are in charge of the investigations into the unfortunate incident at our home last Sunday." She used the Japanese word customarily employed to refer to events of some political significance, like attempted *coups d'état* or mutinies, and Otani was slightly jolted by it.

"That is so, madam," he replied gravely. "Indeed, you may be aware that a member of my staff has already had the benefit of a conversation with your son, as well as interviewing members of the permanent staff of the School."

Mrs Minamikuni opened her gleaming black crocodile handbag to reveal a scarlet satin lining, and produced a packet of Winston cigarettes and a holder. "You don't mind if I smoke?"

"Please go ahead." Otani was taken aback. It was usually only bar hostesses who smoked while dressed in kimono. He had never previously in his life lit a cigarette for a woman, but nevertheless almost without a conscious thought fumbled for matches and did so in this case. It was only afterwards that he felt relieved that Ninja Noguchi had not been there to see him behaving like a hired gigolo in one of the Tokyo "host clubs" patronised by wealthy women or thrill-seeking office ladies on a spree.

He waited for his visitor to continue, but she sat back in her chair, her eyes slightly narrowed, and just looked at him. It was a technique he habitually employed himself, but this time he was the first to give up.

"The reason is quite fortuitous. My wife and I happened to be among the guests at the tea ceremony during which your husband was, er—"

"My husband was accidentally killed," she supplied, still looking quite composed. "Yes, I know you were."

"Under the circumstances, my superiors in Tokyo felt that, since in any case I should have been involved in the enquiry as a witness to what occurred, it might simplify matters if I were to conduct such enquiries as might be necessary."

"I can quite see that, Superintendent," Mrs Minamikuni said. "You are of course a very distinguished and well-known figure in the Kansai area, and we invited you and your wife for that reason. It was fortunate that you were on the spot and could take steps for the protection of His Excellency the British Ambassador. It would have brought unbearable shame on our entire house had the assassin's plan succeeded." She laid her cigarette holder down, took out a tiny lace handkerchief and dabbed delicately at the corners of her eyes, but without actually touching them. "Even though I have been tragically bereaved, I believe that my late husband would have wished to offer himself as a shield. Destiny moves in strange ways."

It was a fine sentiment, like something out of a *kabuki* play, and Otani was for a moment tempted to express his
170

respect in the face of such proud altruism. In the event he merely nodded. "I am inexpressibly shocked by the news that the person responsible was none other than Casey-san. Like everyone else in our family, I was deceived by his apparently earnest desire to study the Way of Tea. Yet we now know that he was simply seeking a convenient means of living in Japan so as to make an opportunity to murder His Excellency. Even while he was staying with us at my late husband's invitation, he made several trips to Tokyo and seemed unwilling to tell us what business he might have there. How we played into his hands by inviting His Excellency to the ceremonies in Kyoto!"

Otani frowned and raised a hand, bringing about a momentary break in the flow. "Forgive me, but I must interrupt you. It is by no means satisfactorily established that Casey-san is even *implicated* in this affair; and it is certainly not thought that he was responsible. May I ask how you have arrived at your opinion?"

Mrs Minamikuni leaned forward, and Otani noticed a pulsing at her throat above the V of her delicate silk underkimono. "I will be very frank with you, Superintendent. Your colleague, Superintendent Fujiwara in Kyoto, is a very old family friend. Quite apart from that, my sister is the wife of the Governor. She and her husband were also guests at that . . . that dreadful occasion. It can hardly surprise you that we have gone over the whole affair between us at very great length. Indeed it was I who was the first to realise that we now had an explanation of the young man's strange behaviour . . . and of some of the things he said to us from time to time. I also remember my late husband saying to me that, although Casey-san showed great promise as a future teacher of the tea ceremony, he felt anxious about his political opinions."

Otani's mind was racing as he was trying to assimilate the implications of everything the woman was saying, and it was imperative not to betray his true feelings. "I see,"

171

he said lamely. "Your testimony is of course highly relevant. Difficulties do remain, however. One purely practical consideration. Surely Casey-san could have had no idea that the ambassador would happen to be visiting the Kansai region at a time convenient for him to be invited to the ceremony? In other words, he could surely have had no guarantee of ever gaining access to His Excellency through, how shall I put it, insinuating himself into the confidence of the Grand Master?"

Mrs Minamikuni assumed a modestly triumphant expression, like that of one about to score a telling point in an argument. "On the contrary," she said. "It is well-known that we *always* invite all the foreign ambassadors to our New Year ceremonies. Perhaps you don't know that we have a branch house in Tokyo. We hold identical ceremonies there the week after they take place in Kyoto, and the British Ambassador as a great expert on Japan always tries to be present. Mr Casey would almost certainly have been invited to assist there this year."

Otani maintained an expression of polite bafflement, and after a moment Mrs Minamikuni continued. "In the case of ambassadors, of course, we always telephone their social secretaries to see if an invitation would be acceptable. His Excellency unfortunately had other commitments during the Tokyo dates, but we were pleased to learn that he planned to be in Kyoto at exactly the right time to honour us by being present at one of the ceremonies there."

"You have given me a great deal to think about, madam," Otani said entirely truthfully. "I am greatly obliged to you for coming forward at this time."

Mrs Minamikuni replaced her cigarette holder in her bag and directed a brave little smile at him. "I just wanted you to know that we would not wish our private grief to stand in the way of our duties as good citizens. As you will appreciate, I shall be totally occupied with the funeral ceremonies tomorrow, so I came today. I thought there were

172

a number of things you ought to know rather urgently."
She stood up, and Otani rose too. Mrs Minamikuni was
standing very close to him and he tried to back away but
was trapped by the arrangement of the chairs.

"After the funeral is over, I should be pleased to help
you in any way I can, Superintendent," she breathed. Her
perfume was as insistent as her manner was blatant. "It
has been a great comfort to meet you. It would be a pleasure to see you again."

Otani side-stepped out of the enclosure of chairs and
regained his freedom. "I thank you again for coming at
such a difficult time for you. I will escort you to the entrance." He bowed, then made for the door and held it
open for her. As Mrs Minamikuni passed through, a wave
of righteous indignation surged in Otani. "Mr Casey is in
a very unhappy situation," he said grimly. "In the face of
accusations against him which in the nature of things it is
virtually impossible for him to rebut."

"Of course he cannot rebut them," Mrs Minamikuni
said equably as they headed towards the staircase, past the
framed photographs of Otani's predecessors on the wall.
"If he belonged to our Japanese tradition he would no doubt
commit suicide as a mark of contrition for his failure to
achieve what he set out to achieve."

Otani's final bow as the widow of the late Grand Master
left the premises was correct rather than courteous.

Chapter 22

ALTHOUGH THE WEATHER IN JAPAN DOES NOT ALWAYS obediently behave in the ways conforming to the time-honoured expectations of the people of that country, the period of so-called "Great Cold" was setting in more or less according to schedule. It was the first night which could truly have been described as downright cold rather than merely chilly, but Inspector Sakamoto braced his wiry shoulders against it with a sense of satisfaction. The great Daitoku-ji complex of Zen temples was not all that far away, and Sakamoto experienced a momentary sense of identity with the monks who would no doubt be at their meditations at such a time; protracted meditations probably since the hardest weather was the time for the greatest austerities. Now that he could live in Kyoto Sakamoto thought that he would try to find a Zen master under whose tutelage he might gain even greater control over his sometimes wayward emotions.

There were other possibilities. The monks of the Tendai sect in their temples high on the snow-covered summit of Mount Hiei to the north-east of the city practised winter

174

disciplines which were no less rigorous than those of the Zen monks in the city below. He might be able to take part in some of them even as a layman. More simply still, there was nothing whatever to prevent him from going down to the spectacular temple of Kiyomizudera any night, changing into a *fundoshi* loincloth and standing under the sacred waterfall reciting sutras while being drenched by one of the three icy cascades whose flow had not varied, winter or summer, for a thousand years and more. He had never yet done it himself, though he had seen others at their spiritual exercises there, the chilling water striking the nape of the neck and pouring down the naked body. It was best to undergo the austerity on a hundred successive nights through the winter months, he knew; though police duty rosters might make that difficult for him to achieve.

It was good to experience again on a day-to-day basis the ineffable sense of rightness which came from being able to serve once more with simple, uncomplicated and perfect loyalty the man to whom he had pledged that loyalty so many years before. Had they both lived in a better, more ordered age, that man could well have been his feudal lord anyway. It was only before and during the war, when he was still too young to savour the situation to the full, that the virtues of unquestioning obedience to His Majesty and to the officers of the armed forces who served his divine will had flowered truly. Everything since then had constituted a chipping away at the foundations of the national polity.

Sakamoto strode on towards his destination, now oblivious to the bite of frost in the air. It was a cloudless, almost sparkling night. The moon was up, and the stars glittered in a jewelled velvet backdrop to the silhouette of the majestic main gate to the temple precincts. Take Otani, for instance. A man of undoubted ability, and with a devious, probing mind. Yet Sakamoto knew him to be at heart an undisciplined sentimentalist. He proceeded not on principle, but in a pragmatic way. He was disgustingly uxorious, deferring to the wife Sakamoto had never met but had heard so much about; a woman it seemed who presumed to hold opinions, and even worse, to give expression to them. He permitted his impertinent familiars Kimura and Noguchi to speak their minds, even encouraging them to do so, and condoned their appalling breaches of discipline.

It all came down to discipline. Sakamoto despised the "soft" postwar image of the police, the idea that they were to protect and befriend the people, and to reproach and reason with obvious criminals, regarding the invocation of the legal process as a last resort, even a kind of failure. In the old days the police had been guardians and mentors of the social order, whose sacred task was to uncover and root out those elements which constituted a potential canker and above all to track down those who harboured "dangerous thoughts" and even dared to question the policies laid down by His Majesty's generals.

It was no wonder that Otani was decadent. His own father had been notorious, a professor of chemistry who had not only openly sided with the criminal Professor Minobe in his vile pre-war allegations that the Imperial Throne of Japan was a mere "organ of the state", but had even attempted with some success to corrupt his jailers during his weeks of confinement, so Sakamoto had heard. There had been many times over the years when Sakamoto had become deeply depressed at the thought that the son of such a man could be placed in a position of authority and influence.

Sakamoto was cheerful that evening, though. Things were going well, and he would soon be able to enjoy the satisfaction of knowing that he had faithfully served the interests of the man to whom he owed his true allegiance. The fact that Otani would have been outwitted and discomfited in the process was a special, personal bonus.

In the very few days since his arrival to join the head-quarters staff of the Kyoto Prefectural Police Force, Saka-moto had already made it his business to visit each of the divisional headquarters in the city proper, and fully intended to do the same elsewhere in the prefecture during the next week or so. All the divisional inspectors in the city had therefore met the new Head of the Criminal Investigation section, and they and their staff had read Superintendent Fujiwara's circular minute advising them of Sakamoto's appointment and instructing them to co-operate with him in every way.

The staff of the Northern Divisional Headquarters in particular already knew him quite well, since he had made several visits there to continue the interrogation of Patrick Casey; and the senior patrolman on duty at the desk jumped up at once as Sakamoto entered through the swing doors. Sakamoto nodded with an approach to affability as the man stiffened and saluted him. He at least seemed to have gathered that the new headquarters inspector was not a man to be treated off-handedly.

"I shall not disturb the senior duty officer. I intend merely to put a few more questions to the foreigner. He has had his evening meal?"

"At the authorised time, sir. Six-thirty."

"And when did the duty officer make his check?" Sakamoto already knew what the answer would be. He had timed his arrival accordingly.

"About ten minutes ago, sir. He should be back before long." The man's face was red and strained, and it gratified Sakamoto to see how thoroughly intimidated he appeared to be.

"You may stand at ease," he said with a small, acid smile. Better and better. He had quite expected to have to receive the key to the lock-up from the duty officer and to have to brush off with a show of comradely good humour the inevitable offer to escort him to Casey's cell.

177

Sakamoto made for the counter flap, which the senior patrolman hastily raised to enable him to pass through. "I know where the key is kept," he said. "If you will just unlock the cabinet for me I will make my own way." The man at the desk was curiously clumsy in his movements, it seemed to Sakamoto. He blundered into a chair on the way to the duty officer's room, and fumbled awkwardly with the bunch of keys chained to his belt before he managed to unlock the simple wooden wall cabinet which contained rows of other keys, each with a numbered plastic tab, hanging on similarly numbered hooks.

Sakamoto tossed Key No. 4 up and down in his hand as he passed to the back of the big general office. There were only a handful of men in it, all patrolmen by the look of them, even two in plain clothes, and they all jumped to their feet as Sakamoto went by. The only person of rank in view was a raw-looking young assistant inspector, a college graduate no doubt and very probably a Communist, Sakamoto thought. Nevertheless, he nodded distantly at the boy, who opened his mouth as though to greet him but then closed it again as Sakamoto proceeded without pause.

It had not been easy to arrange to keep Casey there even as long as they had, and he was due to be moved to Kyoto Prison to the south of the city the next day, where he was to be visited by a member of the staff of the Irish Embassy from Tokyo. Otani had insisted that the very basic facilities at the divisional headquarters lock-up were unsuitable for more than a very few days. Otani again. It was typical of his flabby attitude.

There were only two cells off the corridor at the back of the building, and the corridor itself was dimly lit. Sakamoto had not wished to ask the question openly, so he first went to check whether or not the second cell was occupied. It might very well contain a drunk, even though it was a little early for that. Not that the proximity of a drunk would be anything to worry about. Anyone drunk enough to find

178

himself in the "pig-box" of a Japanese police station would be much too far gone to know what day of the week it was, let alone have the slightest idea what if anything might be happening in the next cell.

In any case, all was well. The low-powered ceiling light glowed in Casey's cell and Sakamoto could see through the Judas hole the young man sitting hunched on his bed, peering in the dim light at a book. The next cell was dark and silent, though; manifestly unoccupied. As he fitted Key No. 4 into the lock and saw Casey start and look towards the door, Sakamoto resolved to find out who had provided him with the book, and why. It seemed to be a wholly unjustified extravagance.

"Oh. It's you," Casey said as he recognised Sakamoto. "You haven't come to try to get me to sign something again, have you? I won't, you know. Not till I've seen somebody from my Embassy." How fortunate it was that the young man spoke Japanese so competently. It would have made Sakamoto's task very much more complicated had that not been the case.

"No," Sakamoto said. "No, nothing like that. Something much simpler." First he drew the new pair of white cotton gloves from his pocket and put them on carefully. They were of the kind frequently worn by taxi-drivers. Then he took from another pocket a four-page leaflet which had struck him as being the most suitable piece of literature for his purpose out of the selection in the rack near the entrance to the Roman Catholic cathedral in the busy Kawaramachi shopping street. It appeared to be concerned with repentance and contrition, and was of course in Japanese, but no matter.

"I realised that you must be in a very precarious frame of mind when you asked me to bring you some Catholic literature, Casey. I understand that your church is opposed to suicide. The foreign priests will not be pleased with you when they discover that your guilty conscience led you to take this step. On the other hand, your Japanese acquaintances will not condemn you for it. Quite the reverse. You will be thought to have done the right thing.''

Casey had backed himself against the wall while Sakamoto was speaking, and looked truly terrified. ''Your belt will do very nicely, Casey. The marks will obliterate any made by me.'' Sakamoto moved swiftly, spun the young man round and seized him from behind, his fingers probing. It was the Zen moment, a total clenching of his body and spirit, and it was as though his hands contained in them all the power of his whole body.

He did not see the bunk bed, slung from the wall by its leather straps, rise up as though it had a life of its own. It was not until huge hands even more powerful than his own seized his wrists and dragged them apart that he first smelt, and then saw, the hated Ninja Noguchi. At the same moment the cell door seemed to cave in.

''Inspector Sakamoto, you are under arrest,'' said Inspector Mihara.

''You left it a bit late, Ninja,'' Otani commented, stepping round the door, which was off the hinges that had been temporarily secured with a pair of trimmed-down chopsticks.

Chapter 23

"THERE'S NO NEED TO TURN THE PLACE UPSIDE down," Otani said, shaking his head in mock despair as Hanae scurried about with a look of almost comical anxiety on her face. She was wearing one of her oldest kimonos, on top of which she had a voluminous old-fashioned apron. Her sleeves were taped back to bare her arms and her hair was protected by a white cloth. "You look like a maid at an inn as it is. It's not the Emperor who's coming, you know."

Hanae ignored him, pointedly tidying once more every part of the downstairs sitting room except the actual corner where he was sitting leafing through his draft report to the Superintendent-General of the National Police Agency. He had brought it home with him to check and revise over the weekend and planned to discuss it with Atsugi of the Foreign Ministry in Osaka the following Monday before submitting it and waiting for the inevitable summons to Tokyo to discuss it.

The Sakamoto aspect of the affair could not possibly be challenged. There as an appendix to the report was the photocopy of his personnel record showing that he had served as a small-arms instructor in the Imperial Army. There too, supplied with some reluctance by the Defence Agency through the good offices of Atsugi, was a copy of his military record extracted from their archives, maintained in respect of all former military men who had been recruited to the reconstructed postwar police force. Sakamoto Masao, sergeant instructor. Awarded a citation as Champion Marksman of his regiment. Even more interesting, assigned as personal driver to Major Ryo Fujiwara during service in Shonan-to, as the Japanese re-named Singapore during the occupation.

Otani's brief career as a junior officer in Imperial Naval Intelligence had been spent wholly in Tokyo, but he knew well enough that Japanese officers in Singapore needed not only drivers but also bodyguards: convenient that Sakamoto could fulfil both functions in respect of his young superior. Fujiwara could only have been in his early twenties himself, but family connections and the appalling death-toll between them had elevated quite a few aristocratic young men to senior rank in the latter stages of the war.

Otani avoided Hanae's flicking feather duster as he glanced again at the duty rosters which showed that Sakamoto had been senior duty officer at Hyogo Prefectural Headquarters on the Saturday night before, and the Sunday night following the killing of the Grand Master, and the statement bearing the seal of the Chief Armourer that the security register indicated that Inspector Sakamoto had carried out personal checks of the weapons held in the basement strong-room on both those days. The Chief Armourer would not admit to a breach of regulations in writing but had readily enough informed Otani that Sakamoto had over the years been a frequent visitor to the training range and had practised not only with hand-guns but also with sharpshooter's rifles of the latest type. Otani had little doubt that it would emerge that Sakamoto had so familiarised himself with the set-up that he could without too much trouble have extracted a rifle on the Saturday and returned it the following night. However much care was exercised over the issue of ammunition, for one or two rounds to go missing was something which could, and no doubt would, be covered up by the Armourer to avoid a fuss. The rifle in question had already been identified by matching it with the shell found by Noguchi among the bamboos.

Most conclusive of all was the tape-recording Noguchi had made of Sakamoto's final conversation with Patrick Casey and the photograph taken by Inspector Mihara as he and Otani broke into the cell while Sakamoto's white-gloved hands were still round Casey's neck. His wild-eyed glare into the camera was in itself almost enough to damn him. Sakamoto had yet to put his seal to a formal confession, but Otani had no doubt that he would before long. Getting him to implicate anyone else would be quite a different matter, though, and Otani sighed.

Hanae misinterpreted the sigh, and whirled round defensively. "I'm sorry, but they *are* due to arrive in half an hour, and I still have to change."

Otani smiled and hauled himself up. "I'm not upset with you, Ha-chan," he said. "I think you've made the place look very nice indeed. I specially like the flower arrangement upstairs. That branch of plum blossom must have cost a fortune. You've got all the food ready, have you?"

Hanae nodded, still defensive. "Yes. I've prepared formal trays for after the tea ceremony. Look, you're not to make a fuss, but I'll be serving the brown rice Rosie-san sent us. You don't have to eat it."

There was no reaction from her husband, and she was emboldened to go on. "It will be really rather nice to use

183

the old tea ceremony things again. They haven't been out of their boxes since Father died, you know.''

Otani nodded. He had found himself unexpectedly moved when retrieving the beautifully crafted wooden boxes from the recesses of one of the cupboards and gently untying the flat silk braids which secured their lids. The lacquer container for the powdered tea and even the tea bowls themselves were of no very great value, but they had been in his family for generations, and it had been something of a disappointment to him when his daughter Akiko had flatly refused to take lessons in the tea ceremony and even Hanae herself had not attempted to maintain after the old man's death the pretence of interest she had kept up during his lifetime. Strange that they were to be used again for the first time after such a long interval by a foreigner of all people, even if he was now an authorised master of the Southern School.

Otani had insisted on that, even before seriously attempting to untangle the extent of the complicity of members of the family in the killing of the late Grand Master. Sitting there quietly, himself already dressed up to please Hanae in his dark-blue kimono of fine wool, the broad silk band of the obi snug about his waist and tied at the back by Hanae in a flat asymmetrical bow, Otani laid his papers down and reflected on the tense formality of the scene he had witnessed the previous day in the venerable ''main house'' in Kyoto. Still pale and drawn from his ordeal, Casey had been the picture of austere dignity in his own formal Japanese dress as he bowed low before the new Iemoto and received from his hands the stiff paper scroll which bore in exquisite brushwork the statement of confirmation that, having been initiated into and diligently studied the Way of Tea in accordance with the precepts of the Southern School, ''Patoriku Keishii'' was duly authorised to teach the art.

Soon they would be at the house, the young tea master
184

and Rosie Winchmore, taking what Otani suspected would be an unauthorised break from her intensive studies at Nanzan University in Nagoya. Well, there was still a tremendous amount to be done, but the clouds had been lifted from the heads of the young people. A monstrous injustice had been done to Casey, but a worse one averted, and Rosie now had an explanation of Otani's previously incomprehensible behaviour towards her. How better to mark their reconciliation than with a tea ceremony at home, followed by some relaxed conversation, plenty of sake and some instant photographs as mementos taken with the camera kindly lent by Inspector Kimura? Otani did not know, but could guess, what the philandering Kimura normally used it for.

Otani looked at his watch, then tidied his papers and put them away in a plain folder at the side of the small table on which stood the television set. Then he made his way upstairs to find Hanae in her silk under-kimono looking indecisively at three different outer ones spread out on the tatami mats around her. "That one," he said promptly, pointing to the one she had worn on the day of the fatal tea ceremony. "It's a festive sort of occasion, after all."

Hanae shook her head. "I don't like to, somehow. Not after what's happened." Then came the thought that clinched the matter. "I can't anyway. Rosie-san has already seen me in it."

"What has that got to do with it?" Otani was honestly baffled, but Hanae wasted no breath in replying to him. Instead she chose a kimono he could not remember having seen before, which depicted the four seasons painted subtly around the hem and on the sleeves on a pale blue background. After all, she must look fully her age in the presence of a woman ten years younger than her own daughter. Then came the choice of obi. She pondered and then her instinct led her to one of her favourites: a fine textured cream brocade with touches of pink.

Otani watched her as she dressed, wondering as always how she managed the complicated process without the aid of a maid or daughter. But then, he supposed, most women had to cope by themselves nowadays. "You must be very pleased," she suggested.

"In a way, yes of course. But Sakamoto was just the instrument. I'm sure of that, even though I'm equally sure that he won't say anything to implicate Fujiwara."

Hanae's eyes widened. "But surely it's obvious to everyone that Superintendent Fujiwara must have been behind it? He's the new Grand Master's real father, after all." Otani had been much more forthcoming with Hanae after the arrest of Sakamoto, and had told her most of what he had found out about the Minamikuni family connections, and of Fujiwara's alleged link with them.

Otani stood near the tokonoma alcove, unconsciously stroking the surface of the polished trunk of a young cryptomeria tree which formed its upright frame. "There's a lot of circumstantial evidence against him, but he hasn't resigned as I would have expected him to. The National Police Agency ought to force his retirement. They could probably do it on health grounds if they want to avoid a public fuss: I'm told he hasn't been well lately. All the same, if Sakamoto simply comes up with some story to the effect that he had a personal grudge against the Grand Master of some kind or another, Fujiwara could still wriggle out. Under a cloud, certainly, but no more."

Hanae was almost finished, and the transformation from harassed housewife to gracious hostess was remarkable. She seldom during their discussions advanced theories of her own, even though in recent years her husband had more and more come to use her as a sounding-board for his own speculations about cases he was concerned with; where

186

previously he had hardly talked about them at all to her. "Well," she said now, "Inspector Sakamoto must have had an accomplice in the room. You told me that yourself."

Otani nodded. "You're right. We've gone over it again and again. I even thought about staging a reconstruction, but there seems to be very little point in it. People who know the tea ceremony well point out that the movements of the person performing it, his position on the tatami-mat, the direction in which he faces and so on are all absolutely prescribed. So if it was just a question of shooting to hit him somewhere in the body it would only be necessary to establish the angle beforehand. No need to see the target at all. To get him in the *head*, though. That would call for very precise timing, and the gunman would need some signal to let him know the exact moment when the tea master was going to bow to the guests. His head would come up a second before theirs, you see."

"It sounds very complicated," Hanae said. She made a final adjustment to her obi, then patted her hair. "Whatever's the matter?" she said then, alarm in her voice. "Don't you feel well?"

Otani was staring at her fixedly, his mouth half open. Then he shook his head violently. "Yes. No. I mean, I'm fine. The *Governor's wife*! Her sister! A transmitter in her obi, or maybe her hair!" As Hanae continued to look blank, Otani began to pace across the room, talking mainly to himself. "Of course, why didn't I think of it before? Women are always fidgeting with their obi, patting their hair and so forth. Nobody would have noticed: the simplest of codes would do. Pat-pat-pat: he's just come into the room. Pat-pat: get ready, he's whisking the tea . . . then . . . NOW! His head's coming up!" Otani smacked one fist into an open hand, a look of triumph on his face.

"Why?" Hanae enquired.

"Why what? What do you mean, why?"

"Why would the Governor's wife be willing to be an accomplice to the murder of her own lover? You did tell me they'd had an affair, didn't you?"

"Yes. According to this secretary girl Kimura seems to have fallen for. There must be something about the atmosphere of that place, you know. Don't you see, there's a very strong motive? Mrs Minamikuni found out about the affair and there was a tremendous row, presumably because she came upon some letters her younger sister had written to the Grand Master. Well, these letters are still in Mrs Minamikuni's possession—a perfect blackmail instrument to use on the wife of a prominent politician, don't you see? And even though it has been suggested that she didn't care about her husband's womanising except in relation to her sister, Mrs Minamikuni could have got to the end of her tether, couldn't she? It seems he regarded every woman he set eyes on as fair game."

Hanae nodded thoughtfully, experiencing a physical frisson as she remembered the look in those eyes, locked on hers for no more than a moment.

"One can feel a certain sympathy with the woman," Otani went on, and Hanae's head snapped up.

"Judging by what you told me about Mrs Minamikuni," she said tartly, "she doesn't need anybody's sympathy."

Otani gave her one of his rare smiles. "All right. But she'd still need someone's help. It's Fujiwara's involvement that bothers me most. Could the Governor's wife have been having an affair with *him*, I wonder? It's funny, you know, Fujiwara never married. Very unusual for a man in his position . . . ." He was interrupted by the ringing of the doorbell, and a look of pure panic spread over Hanae's face.

"*Ara!* They're here already!" she wailed, and fled down the stairs. Hanae had disappeared into the kitchen

188

by the time Otani followed at a more stately pace, arriving in the entrance hall just as the sliding door rattled open.

Feeling something of a fool, Superintendent Tetsuo Otani sank down to his knees to do the honours.

Chapter 24

KNEELING THERE IN THE ROOM THAT HE AND HANAE slept in, Otani felt heartily relieved that Noguchi wasn't there to witness the scene. Not that Patrick Casey's performance of the tea ceremony was an embarrassment: far from it. In the formal dress which became him very well, with his pale face and general air of looking older than his years, he made a picture of cultured refinement as he went through the solemn ritual. His movements lacked the insolent assurance which had been displayed by the late Grand Master in the last moments of his life, but that was scarcely surprising. For all that, he looked every inch the teacher.

Hanae, too, looked gracious, and in her husband's eyes beautiful as she watched intently. The cakes eaten as a preliminary had come from one of the oldest shops in Osaka, and Otani himself had been given the duty of buying the powdered tea on the occasion of what he hoped would be his last visit to Kyoto for some time. He had played safe by choosing the most expensive kind.

It was, alas, Rosie who struck an incongruous note, in

her faded and patched jeans, and a sweatshirt with a curious device and some words printed on it. The Otanis were as skilled in the art of selective vision as any other Japanese, and were quite ready not to notice her clothes, but it was more difficult to disregard the subdued snorts which came from her at frequent intervals as she tried valiantly not to giggle. The really terrible thing was that it was catching, and it needed every bit of Otani's self-control to prevent his own shoulders from heaving as he observed Rosie out of the corner of his eye.

Otani was in any case in a state of euphoria, which had been triggered off by the arrival of the two at the front door. Casey had exuded the very spirit of Kyoto as he bowed low, murmuring the appropriate courtesies, then unobtrusively handed over their present with the prescribed expressions of embarrassment over its inadequacy and general wretchedness. In fact it was a large bottle of the finest "super-special" grade sake: highly satisfactory by any reckoning. Behind Casey, though, Rosie had stood beaming. Her bow was as inelegant as her Japanese, but the sheer goodwill emanating from her had touched Otani, and he was thrown into delighted confusion when she leaned forward and kissed him on the cheek.

He looked at her now in real affection. The badly-stifled giggles had subsided, and there was a preternaturally solemn expression on her freckled face as she accepted the first bowl of tea. Otani and Hanae had both been adamant that she should take the place of honour, and had immediately forgiven her for doing so at once, ignorant of the fact that she should have demurred.

They all watched as she raised the bowl to her lips and sipped, then pulled the most comical face as she tasted the bitter liquid. Casey did no more than smile quietly, busy as he was making the next bowl. This came to Otani, to whom the taste was perfectly familiar. As he drained his tea, wiped the rim of the bowl in the prescribed manner

191

and laid it on the tatami mat in front of him he winked solemnly at Rosie, who went bright red in a successful attempt to suppress another paroxysm of mirth.

Hanae was last, and played her part with deft grace; and soon it was over. They all bowed, and Patrick Casey looked at the little gathering expectantly. Otani turned to Rosie. "You have one more duty, Rosie-san," he said gravely. "As guest of honour, it is for you to thank the sensei on behalf of all of us."

Rosie looked round wildly, and Otani noticed Casey nod at her, the same quiet smile on his lips. "Oh," she said. "Sorry. Yes. Well. Thank you very much, Patrick. It was very interesting. Actually, if you want to know what I think, it's absolutely horrible, and can't be good for you. All that stimulant, I mean."

Since she spoke in English, neither Hanae nor Otani could understand. Casey bowed to them, smiling more broadly, and interpreted. "Rosie-san has expressed most eloquently what is in her heart," he explained. "I have been honoured to perform the tea ceremony for you . . . and I shall never forget what I owe to you, Otani-san."

Now they could all relax, and Otani settled himself more comfortably as Hanae took away the tea bowls and other implements, with Rosie's help. They were soon back, with the lacquer trays of food Hanae had prepared, and plenty of sake, Otani was glad to see. Indeed, after three or four cups, he was emboldened to ask Rosie the significance of the sign on her sweatshirt.

"Oh, that? Campaign for Nuclear Disarmament," she said. "No Cruise Missiles Here. I got it at Greenham Common. That's how I bust up with Roger. Glad I did, now." She grinned hungrily at Patrick Casey, who once more had to render her English into reasonably comprehensible Japanese. A touch of colour came into his own cheeks as he explained that Rosie and Roger, whom he believed they had met in London, were no longer . . . er, that is to say . . . close friends.

Hanae and Otani nodded solemnly, and to cover the momentary embarrassment Otani ate half of his bowl of brown rice without really noticing what he was doing. It was Rosie who then volunteered the news that the newly-qualified tea-master was planning to establish himself in Düsseldorf in Germany, of all places, in order to earn his living by giving lessons to the wives and daughters of the numerous Japanese businessmen living there. She didn't actually say as much, but left the Otanis in little doubt that she planned after graduation to make her way there too. Hanae wanted to ask very discreetly whether she possessed any kimonos, but restrained herself. The self-contained Mr Casey seemed to have the measure of the young lady, and they would no doubt come to some satisfactory, even if only temporary understanding.

The meal was over, and Patrick Casey had begun to make preliminary noises about departing when the telephone rang and Otani went to answer it downstairs. During his absence Hanae referred in a complimentary way once more to Keishii-sensei's elegant outfit, wondering however if he found it a *little* inconvenient as a foreigner to go about in public like that. For the first time the Irishman looked as young as he was, and Hanae could quite see why Rosie might prefer him to Roger.

"My other clothes are in a bag in a locker at the station," he explained, his face alive with amusement. "It isn't easy changing in a tiny toilet in a coffee bar, but I did it on the way here, and I'll do it again after we leave. I've got the same kind of sweatshirt as Rosie—she brought it for me as a present."

It was obviously the right moment to leave, and after only token protests Hanae let them lead the way to the stairs. Otani was half-way up them on his way back from his phone conversation, but retreated again and backed into the living-room until Casey had reached the tiny entrance hall and stepped down into his wooden *geta* sandals. Rosie sat firmly on the wooden step to put on her canvas training shoes, and then they both turned to bow to the Otanis, who were by then on their knees to bid their guests farewell.

The old house seemed very quiet after they were gone and Hanae felt an inexplicable mood of melancholy come over her. She looked up from where she was sitting on a zabuton cushion in the living room as Otani came back into the house from the front gate where he had been standing, waving shyly until Casey and Rosie rounded the corner of the street.

"It was very nice, wasn't it?" she sighed. "But it makes me feel rather old and a little sad."

There was tenderness in his swarthy face as Otani looked down at her. "Why don't you ring Akiko-chan in London and have a little talk with her? Tell her about this evening. It'll be morning there."

Hanae cheered up at once. "Do you know, I think I will," she said, then looked at her husband with some concern. "You look worried. Has something happened?"

Otani shook his head. "Not really. You go and talk to Akiko. I've got things to think about. You see, that was Inspector Mihara from Kyoto on the phone. He's just discovered why Fujiwara's been having so much sick leave for the past few months. It seems he has cancer. It puts things in a rather different perspective."

Chapter 25

"**T**ELL ME HONESTLY," OTANI INSISTED. "HOW MUCH did you know from the beginning?" The members of the Osaka Rotary Club were streaming out of the enormous private room after their luncheon meeting and dispersing into the anonymity of the Royal Hotel, and Atsugi nodded and smiled at a number of them as he placed a strong hand behind Otani's elbow and led him to one side.

"Not very much," he said at last. "It seemed to me to be a strange way to go about killing the British Ambassador, sure. But I didn't deliberately try to steer you away from the Minamikuni family. I'm glad you got that young Irishman out of trouble. How did the visit to your home go?"

Otani smiled reminiscently. "I think my wife lost her heart to Casey," he said. "He seems to have a way with women. The English girl has obviously decided she made a mistake in parting with him the first time. Maybe it's something about tea ceremony masters."

Atsugi nodded. "Could be." Then his big, fleshy face took on a troubled expression. "It's a mess, though. The

195

doctors say that Fujiwara's cancer is pretty far advanced. He has maybe three months. I've talked to the brass in Tokyo and they're inclined to let the marriage go ahead to give him that much comfort at least. After all it begins to look as though it would be hard to prove he had any personal hand in the matter. Who would have thought the Minamikuni woman would have gone on being crazy about him over all those years?''

"It will be that much harder to pull her in later,'' Otani said. "And even when we do, the case against her won't be watertight. We shall get nothing out of Sakamoto, I'm quite sure.'' He shook his head worriedly. Having had several lengthy sessions with Sakamoto, Otani was convinced that his former subordinate was clearly mad. He had confessed to having fired the shot which killed the Grand Master, but insisted that he had acted alone. He would give no explanation of his motive, and denied the existence of a conspirator. Sakamoto also admitted faking the evidence against Casey, and attempting to murder him and make it appear that he had committed suicide. The theory that there had been an attempt to assassinate the British Ambassador had provided him with the idea, and with the opportunity to sacrifice the young man, concerning whom Sakamoto showed no remorse whatever. He seemed, in fact, to have entered a condition of almost mystical serenity, and Otani despaired of making any more progress through interrogation.

Atsugi rubbed his nose. "We did what you asked. We made very discreet but very thorough enquiries. There's no doubt whatever that the Governor's wife has had an affair with the Iemoto within the past five years, and it seems very possible that her elder sister has been blackmailing her in some way. Psychologically it wouldn't have been difficult. Apparently when they were young the two sisters were inseparable and the younger one was completely under the thumb of the elder. As to whether the new Grand

Master is really Fujiwara's son, only Mrs Minamikuni can really tell us the answer, and I somehow doubt if she will. In short, your theory *might* just hold water, Otani-san. All the same, I wouldn't try to prove it if I were you."

He looked at his watch. "Hey, I have to go. Look, I can't stop you arresting Mrs Minamikuni. You're the cop, not me. I don't think you'd find the District Prosecutor would be too pleased, though. It makes a fine magazine story. Childhood lovers, prevented from marrying. A forced marriage, a love child, divorce out of the question in such a family. Widowhood the only hope." Atsugi looked at Otani, one eyebrow raised. "Who knows, perhaps you could dredge up failed attempts on her husband's life during the years. Driven to desperation when lifelong lover develops cancer, plots to kill husband by blackmailing sister and with the willing cooperation of the one man she knows who would do anything without question to serve the interests of the wartime commander he worshipped— and just happened to have the right skills."

Atsugi paused, clapped Otani on the shoulder and left his hand there for a moment. "A great story. Would make a great movie. They could have Toshiro Mifune play the Fujiwara part. But *where's the evidence*, my friend? You got the murderer, after all. I have to go. The British Ambassador's due in town this afternoon. I'll see you."

He turned away, then came back and spoke in a stage whisper. "Know what? He's had another threatening letter. I think he writes them himself."

ABOUT THE AUTHOR

James Melville was born in London in 1931 and educated in North London. He read philosophy at Birkbeck College before being conscripted into the RAF, then took up schoolteaching and adult education. Most of his subsequent career has been spent overseas in cultural diplomacy and educational development, and it was in this capacity that he came to know, love, and write about Japan and the Japanese. He has two sons and is married to a singer-actress. He continues to write more mystery novels starring Superintendent Otani.

The *Insouciant* Wit
of
JAMES MELVILLE

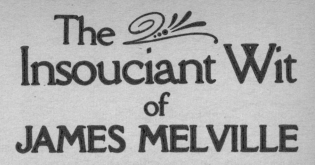

Humor at banal pretense, and an eye for the subtlety of a well planned execution, with a complex plots to ensure suspense fans great pleasure from the Superintendant Otani Series.